Colburn Mayne

Strawberry Hill

And Other Poems

Colburn Mayne

Strawberry Hill
And Other Poems

ISBN/EAN: 9783337416379

Printed in Europe, USA, Canada, Australia, Japan

Cover: Foto ©Andreas Hilbeck / pixelio.de

More available books at **www.hansebooks.com**

STRAWBERRY HILL:

And other Poems.

BY

COLBURN MAYNE.

LONDON :
(FOR THE AUTHOR,)
JOHN CAMDEN HOTTEN, 74 AND 75, PICCADILLY.
1868.

DEDICATION.

TO FRANCES, COUNTESS WALDEGRAVE.

TEN years ago will reach the time
   I saw beneath the surly skies
   Of dim November ghastly rise
The walls that won my rhyme.

Stained o'er by years' and ruin's traces,
   I saw gleam through the antique grove
   The home that won so much of love
And eighteenth century praises.

How sad that wrecked and wasted whim
   Of him, the witty and the wise,
   Who bade the Gothic galleries rise
For Thames to fondly limn!

What loving labour's skill he brought,
  What treasures fetched from famous lands,
  What thought of brain and toil of hands
Went to the work he wrought !

There lived he happy 'neath its roof,
  And gladly worked from year to year ;
  How proud when from its press appear,
The printer saw his proof.

Beneath the roof where now reposes
  Their pictured grace that grows not old,
  Once swept the gracious garments' fold
Of Reynolds' three rich roses.

And mirth and wit and beauty's rays,
  And Selwyn's jest and Wortley's punning,
  Buzzed round the steps of each fair Gunning
In those Walpolian days.

How sad could prophet ray have shone,
  And flashed the future on his mind,
  And shown him scattered all he shrined,
'Ere sixty years were gone !

And yet 'twere worth the bitter sting
 Such flash had sent to heart and brain,
 Had it revealed the future's gain
From future loss to spring.

What rapture then his heart might swell,
 To see the renovated fane—
 See Strawberry's turrets rise again,
And "bear away the bell."

O, Lady, blest be thou, whose thought
, Not lightly, noblest task conceiving,
 With genial taste thy work achieving,
Hast to perfection brought

The halls whose famous Gothic screen
 Gleams brightly as of yore it gleamed,
 When Walpole in his study dreamed
Otranto's wondrous scene.

There, 'midst thy statesmen, wits, and sages,
 Move thou orbed round with all their fame,
 And worthier poets send thy name
To live through coming ages.

PREFACE.

Should any one, having glanced at my volume, ask me, " Do you imagine that there is a place for this on the shelf that holds the works of such poets as Tennyson, Browning, Arnold, Morris, and Swinburne ?" I would at once answer, " No."

But then, such question would presume some competition between my book and the writings of these men, and this would be indeed to mistake my aim, which was simply to tell, as well as I could, the tale of a place which, standing near my own birthplace, and surrounded by the scenes I have loved from childhood, has ever been regarded by me with a yet deeper and tenderer interest than that which it must possess for every lover of the literature of the last century.

It seemed to me that the tale of " Strawberry Hill," often already told in prose, might be yet better told in verse, and that the verse best adapted to such a tale

would be that which, avoiding all approach to passion
or profundity, should aim at being merely a lengthened
form of the *vers de société*.

To preserve this from unnecessary tedium, a frequent change of metre and—as often as possible—of
subject, seemed requisite, and this — how far suc-
cessfully, others must judge—I have endeavoured to
introduce.

Around the central subject of my rhyme I have
sought to group my favourites—the men and women of
the days of Sir Joshua Reynolds; the men and women
who have been looking down on us from his canvas
for the past two years at the National Portrait Exhibition—Sir Robert Walpole and his beautiful bride;
their son Horace, the Lord of Strawberry; Horace's
three fair nieces, the offspring of the romantic love of
Edward Walpole and Mary Clements, one of whom,
having married the Earl of Waldegrave, became the
mother of those three still more renowned beauties,
Horatia, Maria, and Laura Waldegrave, whose portraits, by Sir Joshua Reynolds, long familiar to some
in the gallery at Strawberry Hill, were, last year,

exhibited to the public at the National Exhibition.
These, with their fair contemporaries, the Cummings
and Lady Mary Wortley Montague, and others just
glanced at, floated before my vision, and seemed to
allure me to endeavour to fasten them on my page.

Conscious as I am how blurred are the outlines and
misty the lights of my portraits, I yet hope that some
may glance, not altogether unfavourably, at this
attempt to represent a few of the brilliant figures of
the last century as they may have peopled the rooms
and enlivened the lawns of " Strawberry Hill."

With regard to the minor pieces in this volume,
they are dear to me because they mirror much of a
time that, till I had written all but the last of them, I
knew not was so soon to pass from me.

Almost perfect happiness is in this world so rare,
that, perhaps, they will please by their picture of a
life that seemed nearly to touch upon it, while to me
they will ever be the record of the days

" So fair. so fresh, the days that are no more."

CLEVELAND SQUARE, *May.* 1868.

CONTENTS.

MISCELLANEOUS POEMS.

STRAWBERRY HILL

CANTO I.

SIR ROBERT WALPOLE.

1.

THE WEDDING.

July's last eve, and William king,
  The century scarce eight months begun,
And all men wondering would it bring
  Vast changes e'er the year were run;
A quiet Norfolk village, where,
  The toils and heat of labour o'er,
The men in little knots repair
  To argue round the ale-house door.
, Such is the time, and such the scene
  On which 1 bid the curtain rise;
The old oak-tree—the village green—
  The sailing clouds of summer skies.

B

Some gossipped of the failing strength
   Of that great man who ruled the realm,
And others, " Well, 'tis time at length
   That English hands should take the helm :
The Princess, bless her ! she, you know,
   Was born amongst us, English bred,
To me 'twill be no day of woe
   That sets the crown upon her head ;
The Dutchman may be called away,
   Whene'er God sees it to be best,
Though, while he lives, I, too, will say,
   ' God save King William' with the rest."
"Well, neighbour, well, sure, you forget
   Our king's great soul—his glorious deeds—
One in a million, he who set
   Us free from all their foreign creeds,
Who fought King Lewis and the French ;"—
   But, hark ! the bells ring sudden out,
And gossips on the ale-house bench
   Break off to see what 'tis about ;
And soon the rumour rose and spread,
   And buzzed from cottage-door to door,
That yestermorn " Young Squire " was wed,
   That eve his bride he homeward bore.
And now the carriage comes in sight,
   Afar the scarlet jackets gleam,
Snowed on the breast with favours white,
   That badges of his conquest seem—

That good old custom, English quite,
  Which sets such value on the prize,
That he who wins it thinks it right
  To trophy it before all eyes.
So thus, in light of summer day,
  Young Walpole brought his Catherine home,
And Houghton Hall before them lay,
  Instead of Paris or of Rome.

II.

HOUGHTON HALL.

How fair old Houghton looked that eve!
  How rich the acres spread around!
How glad the home that soon must grieve
  The loss of one—one ever found,
In those old days of honest worth,
  A piece of Nature's darling plan,
Her highest standard for the earth,
  A simple sterling Englishman,
Who now stood forth to welcome there,
  With all a father's hearty pride,
The son to Houghton's acres heir,
  The bridegroom with his blushing bride;
And there the servants ranged and ranked,
  And there the tenants trooping all,
With roses and with ribands pranked,
  Shout " Welcome home to Houghton Hall."

A moment turned the bride's sweet face
  In thanks upon the cheering crowd,
The evening gained a gentler grace,
  The joy-bells rang more sweet and loud
As, led across the threshold, she
  Was clasped once more to his strong breast,
And felt, half pained, the kisses he
  Upon her lips in welcome pressed.
Ah, happy days at Houghton Hall,
  Ah, honeymoon of perfect bliss!
How oft, when famous, he'll recall,
  And deem no year so dear as this;
Though on its close swift shadow came,
  Dark falling where the old man slept,
Who, hall and boroughs, wealth and name,
  His father's trust had safely kept
For him, who, kneeling by his grave,
  Felt buried in it lay the flowers
Of those young years he freely gave,
  With their first-fruit of college hours—
That spring of life, whose flushing flame
  Through all youth's pulses swiftly shoots,
And helps the blood in boyhood's frame
  To ripen manhood's gracious fruits—
Those student days, whose golden cup
  O'erflows with the old classic wine,
Whose youth is free with gods to sup
  And drink, rose-crowned, with the divine

Old thinkers, whose sweet Latin lays
Sound echoing from the vales afar
With chime of Cytherea's praise,
Or hymn to the young Julian star—
The days when St. John came to spend
With him his idle hours of college,
And friend, unjealous, brought to friend
The genial help of diverse knowledge ;—
From these, and all that they foretold
Of student honours, student fame—
The future's brilliant chart unrolled
And glittering proudly with his name—
Turning, while now his sight could hail
The goal in view, he left the race,
Came home to quaff the Norfolk ale,
And hunt the deer in Houghton Chace.
And now these roses softly fall,
And whitely o'er his father's sleep,
While he, the whitest rose of all,
An unstained heart may blameless keep ;
Though even now he longs in truth
To wear again, as he has worn,
And blend with his gay rose of youth,
The laurels duty had forsworn.
Now springs again his college dream,
As in his breast ambition woke,
And burned to take up Sidney's theme,
And speak the words that Sidney spoke.

III.

THE STATESMAN.

Beauteous as, seen through some grey arch
  Of Ponte Vecchio, the skies,
And sunlit flash of Arno's march
  Look in the lover's lingering eyes,
So, from the strong stern life that now
  O'erbends our hero's stirring years,
As soft the landscape's tender glow
  That sleeps round Houghton Hall appears;
But, as the hurrying steps of men,
  And life's loud chorus swelling round,
Impel the loiterer on again
  To reach the goal where he is bound;
So Walpole dare not linger now
  Upon the threshold of his fame,
Lest laurels wither on his brow,
  Lest dimmed the radiance of his name;
And steadily, from year to year,
  With stronger lustre seemed to wax
The star of him men named the peer
  Of Compton, Stanhope, Halifax;
But nobler friendship he won then
  In his whose friendship honour gave;
The handsomest of handsome men,
  And of brave soldiers the most brave;
And though, great Churchill, in this age
  Of petty motives, pettier men,

They write thy life, but blot the page
　With slanders on thy name,—what then?
That name shall still throughout all story
　Be held the greatest England had,
And they who strive to mar its glory
　Scarce wicked deemed, but simply mad;
Twin stars, henceforth, of field and State,
　They waxed and waned henceforth together,
Shone brightest through the clouds of hate,
　And steadiest in the roughest weather.
And we, who safely dwell to-day
　Within our wisely tempered land,
Where, on each open ordered way,
　Walk Law and Freedom hand in hand—
Shall we forget to whom we owe
　More than to Fox our happy times,
Leave Marlborough's memory to the foe
　To blacken in sarcastic rhymes?
"Marlbrook se va t'en guerre," they sing;
　Has England learnt no nobler lay,
No mighty anthem burst to fling
　Rich music o'er his glorious clay?
O, rise, some poet's heart of fire—
　Rise to the grandeur of the theme,
With his great name enchant thy lyre,
　And waken fools from their sick dream—
The hope of Laudian days restored
　With hocussed chalice, mimicked rite,

The play at priestcraft men abhorred,
　Who lived in dawn of Freedom's light—
Do ye, who praise the Stuart cause,
　And slander England's noblest king,
Who prate of James's tolerant laws,
　And back your "good old times" would bring,
Forget such hope, now but a dream ;
　Then woke a flame, well fed by Rome,
Till France saw Marlborough's sword gleam,
　And Walpole stamped it out at home ?
When St. John—all their youthful days
　Of student friendship long outgrown—
When Harley subtly sought to raise
　The banished race to England's throne,
Came Marlborough with his glittering fame,
　Came Walpole with his zeal unfeigned,
The nation's heart caught up their flame,
　And Guelphic George in England reigned.

CANTO II.

HORACE WALPOLE.

I.

THE THAMES.

O ROYAL Thames, whose windings flow
  Through many a landscape world renowned,
What beauties has the earth to show
  Like those with which thy banks are crowned?
Wind on by Godstow's ivied wall—
  Wind on by Rosamunda's bower,
From Nuneham's chestnuts o'er thee fall
  Their waxen blooms in summer's shower;
By many a mill, and bridge, and farm,
  Glide thou, reflecting each fair scene;
Dash o'er each weir thy mimic charm
  Of falls that ape a threatening mien.
Then soft the Berkshire meadows lave,
  And Cuyp-like glass in every fold,
The cattle stooping o'er thy wave,
  The summer sunset's lingering gold;

But pause awhile, still loitering where
    Thy curves are wooed by Datchet meads,
'Mid pastures sweetening all the air
    With clover, where the brown bee feeds,
For here thy cunning coils are caught,
    'Midst islets fringed on every side
By trees that bend as though they sought
    To chain thy half-reluctant tide ;
And here, amidst the landscape, rises
    The long-drawn screen of Windsor's keep ;
And here, a link 'twixt Cam and Isis,
    Old Eton's Gothic cloisters sleep.
A century and a half have fled,
    Nor altered one of these fair scenes,
Though all who gazed on them are dead,
    The kings and princes, lords and queens,
Since side by side, in Eton fields,
    Two, deep in youth's delicious themes,
Walked, sharing all that boyhood yields
    Of eager hopes and ardent dreams ;
There, pacing by Thames' flowered sides,
    They paint all life one gay romance,
While Hope holds up the future's slides
    Rose-coloured to their eager glance ;
And they believe that friendship still
    Will follow them through all their days,
And Love a golden cup will fill,
    And still deserve her poet's praise.

II.

THE FRIENDS.

The boy's first friendship formed at school,
　First, purest love we feel in life,
Could all be measured by its rule ;
　How free our after years from strife,
Something there seems almost divine,
　In the pure bond such young lives linking.
O, well writes one, "Such is life's wine,
　And woman's love is but dram-drinking."*
Such love was theirs, who bent away
　From cricket, football, boat, and barge,
'Midst some Arcadian scene to stray,
　On some Arcadian theme enlarge,
To sketch a future, wherein they
　Should soar above their youthful band,
And flash the names of Thomas Gray
　And Horace Walpole through the land.
Perchance on some mild eve in May,
　When garden-thickets gave their scent
Of lilac and of hawthorn spray,
　With the rich meadow-perfumes blent,
They may have paused beside some stream,
　Whose little current stole away
Its waters through the woods to dream,
　In haunts where footsteps seldom stray,

* Lord Lytton.

And gazing on the silver flow,
　One may have wished his life could be
Calm as the stream, and, wishing so,
　Have claimed his comrade's sympathy;
While he, whose fancies spread their wings,
　And fly to London's brilliant scene,
Half gay, half serious, turns and sings
　The thoughts whose language may have been—

　　Give me life not smooth and placid
　　　As that calmly-curving stream,
　　Nor for me existence as it
　　　Reads in your idyllic theme.

　　Be the Thames the chosen river
　　　On the chart you trace for me,
　　With its emblems of endeavour,
　　　With its voice of victory.

　　Grand, majestic, solemn sweeping
　　　On its ever-varied march;
　　Now in summer meadows' keeping,
　　　Now rolled 'neath dark city arch;

　　Now the swan's soft sailing glassing,
　　　Now the mirror of that fleet,
　　Whose loud thunder heard in passing,
　　　Banded Europe fears to meet.

Give me life that mirrors as it
  Palace, prison, fort and fleet,
Church, and mill, and farm-house placid,
  Arching bridge, and thronging street.

From its birthplace gladly springing,
  Sings it like a child along,
Meets a myriad streamlets, bringing
  Their sweet chorus to its song.

Then in currents deeper, wider,
  Gaining manhood's strength and voice,
Gallops, like a gallant rider,
  To the lady of his choice.

So the river to the ocean,
  River wave to ocean tide,
Ever springs with glad emotion,
  As the bridegroom to the bride.

III.

AT COURT.

So may have sung—while blent the words
  With hum of bee and blackbird's strain,
With song of stream and lowing herds—
  His prophecy not all in vain,

The lad who, leaving Eton, went
　　Through every scene of that Court life,
Where dwelt, as in their element,
　　The statesman, Walpole, and his wife—
Where round him glittered the bright rays
　　Of wits and statesmen, beaux and belles,
The Herveys, Swifts, and Popes, and Gays,
　　The Bellendens and young Lepels—
Here Cowper's brilliant Frenchman came,
　　Here reigned the royal Caroline;
Here she shone out in sudden fame,
　　Who once had sold her locks to dine.
Within her magic circle drawn
　　Come half the sages, all the wits,
And Swift is decent as in lawn,
　　And Pope in playful humour hits
That handsome Hervey, whom in time
　　He will defame in vilest verse,
In that detested, loathsome rhyme,
　　Whose memory is its author's curse.
Here Chesterfield attained that grace,
　　Which gave its stamp to half the age;
Here star-like shone that lovely face,
　　Which every passion seemed to cage;
Whose loveliness failed to disarm
　　His satire, or save from his aim,
Who in his vile attempt to harm,
　　For ever sullied his own fame.

Soon that small room where these repaired,
  O'ertòpt the fame of that Greek mount,
Whose goddesses the wits declared
  Would be to-day of small account.
Next those three Maries, whose fair faces
  All lights and shades of beauty dapple,
Till none dare say which of these graces
  Deserves the English shepherd's apple ;
And 'mid this laughing motley crew,
  This air of satire and lampoon,
The Eton stripling's boyhood grew,
  And hastened towards his manhood's noon
That brilliant noon which colour took
  From many a sweet surrounding grace,
The wit of Court, the college book,
  The softness of a mother's face,
That ceased to smile just as his part
  In life the boy should take with men,
And left that death-chill on his heart
  No sun in life could warm again ;
But over many a grave the May
  Will steal with gentle, gradual tread,
And moss, and blossom, and flowery spray
  Will brighten earliest round the dead ;
And sun of May through painted pane
  Will find out where each tomb reposes,
Its sculptured snow carnation stain,
  And flush its lilies into roses.

So, o'er those graves within the heart,
    That fondest memories closely fold,
Life's May will blossom, and fair Art
    Shed beauty with her magic gold;
And thus his youth broke into bloom,
    Thick as the May-tide's regal show,
When all the orchard-buds o'erfoam
    The bending branches with their snow,
As spring-sap thrills those orchard trees,
    So thrills the blood throughout his veins,
Desires aroused Life's zither seize,
    And smite it into nobler strains,
Wed to a song of ampler range,
    While his heart hangs upon the chords,
And youth's impetuous wish for change
    Finds shaping in these wailing words—

Yet a moment I am weary, let my swimming brain find
    rest,
Let my fevered heart throb lower in my vext and
    harassed breast.

I am bound to Life's conventions, as the mill-horse to
    the mill,
Tracking weary circles round it, circle after circle
    still.

All the way is trod down dusty, gone its verdure and
    its flowers,

O, I cannot rest for thinking of the bright untrammelled
hours

That fly before me in the future, up a long and shining
track,
Lit with sheen of snowy pinions, and white garments
floating back;

And my heart strains ever after on the path that they
have gone,
Like the yearning in the coverts of a young deserted
fawn,

Whose eyes are straining sadly with their soft, pathetic
speech,
Seeking vainly for his mother, bounding far beyond his
reach.

So my heart strains to the future, to the hours that it
stores,
To the fair and foreign countries, to the bright and
distant shores.

All the world that lies around me seems a disenchanted
scene,
Scarce believing now is left me in the brightness that
has been.

Eton play-fields, ye were merry; Eton friends, ye once
were dear;

C

But a numbness takes my heart-strings, and all life
    seems dull and drear.

As a fairy banished for an æon from the flower-brimming
    wood,
Creeps to die within its thickets, finds a brick-field
    where it stood ;

So to me those Eton meadows seem but fields for
    common uses,
And from friends that would throng round me I turn
    off with sick excuses.

All the meadow-blossoms faded, all the schoolboy
    friendships cold,
Ah! the world's dust thickens round me, and my heart
    is faint and old!

College cloisters lose their charming, college wit has
    lost its skill,
For my life is out of tuning, and all things seem sad
    and ill.

All the wit has fled from satire, and it only keeps its
    sting;
Pointless are the poisoned arrows that the wittiest
    writers fling.

Spreads the brilliant lore of scholars in long rows from
    shelf to shelf;

I turn from all that it can teach to the reading of
    myself;

Brooding ever o'er that study, till my heart grows faint
    and sick—
Till my brain grows dull and giddy, till the air grows
    close and thick.

Oh, let me 'scape the present, whose stern moments are
    my jailers;
Set my thoughts adrift, and follow them, the future's
    daring sailors.

Let them bear me over oceans, that divide the sad to-
    day
From the future's bright to-morrow, from the traveller's
    golden way.

Let me fly this narrow island, all its life of Court and
    town;
Through the future's free savannahs let me hunt
    adventures down.

Let me climb the Alpine mountains, let me breast their
    snowy heights;
Barriers rising to divide me from fair Italy's delights.

O, Italia, fair Italia, cherished land of proud renown,
Haste the vision's bright fulfilment of each old historic
    town.

c 2

Let me greet thy beauteous Milan, let me walk by
    Arno's side,
Let me see the Lily City glass herself within its tide.

Let me glide through Venice alleys, let me see Rialto
    rise,
Let my spirit sob and shudder 'neath the darksome
    Bridge of Sighs.

Lo, the wide Campagna's desert!—lo, the golden dream
    of years!
Points the driver—shouts exulting—San Pietro's dome
    appears!

Such my spirit's weary waiting for the glad and golden
    time,
That will answer to the visions I but conjure up in
    rhyme.

    Such shaping into mournful rhymes
        Of the heart's yearnings and its sighs,
    Is but the mask youth wears at times,
        But happiness in sorrow's guise.
    Yet all in youth's fair fallow hours
        Have breathed or felt that plaintive strain,
    Though mantled to the lips in flowers
        That fading, never bloom again;

And all like him have longed to fly
　To the world's scenes of old renown,
See glow beneath their golden sky
　Italia's classic tower and town—
Have longed to read the Mantuan's verse,
　Beneath the shade of Mantuan beech,
And hear old Ovid love rehearse,
　Where lingers phrase of Latin speech.

At length life strikes that hour for him,
　He sets his willing sails,
And following only Fancy's whim,
　Strikes out with favouring gales.
And to the youth thus flushed with joy,
　A friend his classics lent,
And, wise with years, as to a boy,
　These kindly verses sent—

Take, my boy, these royal thinkers,
　Go with them 'neath haunted sky;
Drink, as suits all eager drinkers,
　Of the old divinity.
You are flushed with bloom of youth,
　While my bloom has faded long;
Not for me, but you, in sooth,
　Should be classic poet's song.

Take my Virgil, I have read him
　On his native Mantuan ground,

How his hero's wanderings led him
    Half the ancient world around;
But I turned in days of summer
    To the poet's pastoral rhyme,
Broken through with brown bees' murmur,
    As they feasted on the thyme.

Ah! the purple on the cover
    Of my Homer's lost its hue;
It has gone all Europe over
    With me, as it may with you;
And my life has faded faster,
    Since I read those wondrous themes—
Since thy purple, O my master,
    Matched the purple of my dreams.

Ah, my poet boy! thou bringest
    Thoughts and dreams long fled from me,
To these golden rhymes thou stringest
    All thy soul's glad melody;
Gazing on thy glowing present,
    I would quit the paths of men,
Unregretting, for that pleasant
    Lost land of my youth again.

But, as that knows no returning,
    To thy youth I give its dower;
Take, my boy, from classic urning,
    Treasures for each glowing hour.

Take my Virgil—take my Homer,
    Freely read the ancient verse ;
Gladly to each reverent comer,
    The old tales they will rehearse.

You will see the white vests gleaming
    Through the olive-garden's shade ;
You will sleep with Muses, dreaming
    In the Muses' haunted glade.
The old sages will instruct you
    In their philosophic lore,
And their master-minds conduct you
    Over realms they've trod before.

But for me such dreams are over,
    All my classic wanderings past ;
Like Ulysses, the spent rover
    Rests within his home at last ;
And the strains that sound the sweetest,
    Come in phrase of English speech ;
And the poets now the meetest,
    In the English accents teach.

I resign my Homer to you,
    But for that the closer clasp
Wild Will. Shakspeare, happy, so you
    Will not force him from my grasp.
I am not so held in haven
    That I may not go with him,

By the silver urns of Avon,
  By the haunted river's brim.

I am able yet to wander
  With my Pope by Thames's side,
And to watch its currents yonder
  Under the five arches glide.
These are peaceful pleasures, matching
  With the autumn of my days,
With the eye grown dull with watching,
  With the lip that's slow to praise.

Let your ardent youth be fed on
  Nectar, by the ancients given;
Let your burning thoughts be sped on
  Grecian wings to Greece's heaven.
These that make with youth glad blending,
  Match but ill with riper age—
That has long since reached the ending
  Of young Life's ecstatic page.

And when life is ebbing faster,
  And the evening shadows close,
When for me nor pleasant pasture,
  Nor the garden's summer rose;
But, instead, the safest corner
  Of the parlour-fire holds me,
Till e'en Pope may be a scorner
  Of the quiet life that folds me;—

Then my Milton safe will bring me
    On the holy path he went,
And his one true God will sing me
    With no triple visions blent ;
When my eyes are closing slowly
    On the lovely scenes of earth,
He will give me visions holy
    Of a far exceeding worth.

So your classic authors hold them,
    With their roses crown your youth,
In your rapturous visions fold them,
    Let their fable grow to truth ;
But for me life's sober ending
    Claims a higher, holier theme,
Needs a hope of nobler tending
    Than the pagan poet's dream.

In later years, when all that time
    Of joyous voyaging had fled,
With books returning rhyme for rhyme,
    His heart thus sorrowed for one dead.

Take your books—the classic volumes—
    I have tried them all—
The sweet rhymers who have answered
    To my spirit's call.

Once I lisped their magic numbers
　　In my father's ear;
Whisper now or speak them loudly,
　　He will never hear.

Since I've read for Memory's sake
　　All the books he taught me,
I have quaffed the poet's wine
　　By Bacchantes brought me.

Homer's golden lines have floated
　　Down the antique page,
With their grand spondaic echo
　　Of that grander age.

I have wandered down the ages
　　With your wise Ulysses,
Yearning ever for his homestead,
　　And his wife's caresses.

With your Æschylus I've wandered
　　From the purple vine,
Where old Bacchus first possessed him
　　With the juice divine.

I have joined in dance of Hellas,
　　And the Dorian chorus;
While loud the people's plaudits rose,
　　And the god fell o'er us.

Sweet as from the church bells sprinkled
 Come the Christmas chimes ;
Soft as golden dews have fallen,
 Virgil's liquid rhymes.

Yet from these my spirits wander,
 Sad, and faint, and worn,
Knowing that to such rich nurture
 They were never born.

Once I worshipped the old writers,
 Now my pale lips falter ;
O, for some kind hand to lead me
 To a milder altar !

I am sick with gazing ever
 On Jove's blinding splendour ;
Let my drooping eyelids open
 On a light more tender.

Lead me to the English meadows,
 Near the water's fall,
Where the summer calm is broken
 By the cuckoo's call.

Milky hawthorn, purple lilac,
 Give them to my hand ;
Let me scent the dear narcissus
 Of my English land.

Let me hear the oxen lowing
    In our English fields;
Dearer this than all the music
    Classic poet yields.

This is sweet to all my senses—
    Sweet the summer breeze,
Fetching music from the summits
    Of the old elm-trees.

Sweet to me the oxen lowing,
    And the brown bees' hum—
Sweet the summer breezes blowing
    As they go and come.

Over Hybla's fragrant blossoms
    Bees no longer fly;
Pæstum's roses all have faded
    With an age gone by.

Virgil's lilies send a perfume
    Very faint and dead;
Floating withered down the current
    Of the Æons fled.

But the roses smell as sweetly
    From yon wayside hedge,
And the mignonette is fragrant
    On my window's ledge.

Ah! but even as I praise them,
　All their perfume goes ;
And this English rosebud seemeth
　Dead as Pæstum's rose.

Why is this, my English blossoms,
　That ye lose your charm,
While my spirits sink as sudden
　As an unnerved arm ?

Ah ! for this that never landscape,
　Fed by English skies—
Never blossom kept its beauty
　Long in lovely eyes—

Eyes that vainly look around them
　For a dead one's gaze ;
Lips that vainly seek his echoes
　Of their ardent praise.

This was in later years his lay,
　Who then with youth's impetuous joy
Leapt lightly o'er each lovely way
　That marks thy mountains, fair Savoy ;
And, as he rose, beneath him lay
　A house and vine, not famous yet,
Nor pilgrim trod the shaded way
　That led to Rousseau's " Les Charmettes,"

To where, 'neath shade the walnuts wove,
  Dwelt, heedless of all others, they
Who knew no rule of life but love—
  De Warens, Rousseau, young Anet.
Warens, how strange that life of thine,
  Whose verse to pagan tunes was set,
Where still the Lampsacene found shrine,
  And hymns arose to Venus yet;
And yet, where goodness kept the flame
  Of Christian charity alive,
Within a heart, where thronging came
  All virtues save the one to thrive.
And thou, dear youth, the young Anet,
  Whom Nature seemed to mark for fame,
What lovely idylls ever stray,
  And breathe their sweetness round thy name!
The very soul of goodness dwelt
  Within thy young but pensive heart.
For thee a Milton might have felt
  The love that woke the poet's art;
O'er thee, as o'er his Lycidas,
  His reddest roses might have strewed,
And sent thy name to visit us,
  Linked to his verses' sweetest mood.
Yet scarce a lovelier idyll he
  Could waft upon the summer air,
Than Rousseau wove, young Claude round thee,
  In those transparent pages, where

The walnut-trees still seem to wave,
　　The three fond friends to live once more,
And Anet climb where Jura gave
　　To the young peasant all his lore.
Within their little circle locked—
　　Their wishes, cares, their hearts were one,
Their lives at worldly maxims mocked,
　　And what each wished by all was done.
Perchance the century's swing has brought
　　A wiser rule—a better age,
And we prefer the lessons taught
　　In Cresswell's court to Rousseau's page.
I dare not judge, but still sometimes
　　To me our social air grows thick,
Though even then 'tis but in rhymes
　　I care to own, my heart is sick
Of all Convention's shaven lawns,
　　Her velvet ways and close-clipt hedges—
Her scenery, where no morning dawns,
　　All gas-lit seen from opera ledges—
Her stage performance, all whose men
　　Speak cut and dry their studied speech;
And few will dare, scarce one in ten,
　　To move but as their leaders teach ;
And then to me the air blows fresh
　　From far Savoy and Les Charmettes;
I sigh to rend our social mesh,
　　And go 'midst peasants and forget

The laws that chain our lives, and fetter
    Each bright emotion of the soul,
And think I should be wiser—better,
    My life more lovely, on the whole.
Savoy!—what breeze of youth that word
    Blows with a laugh right in my face
From the bright days, when o'er thy sward
    I leapt with all a stripling's grace.
Shall I e'er see thy plains again,
    And brown my cheek in autumn's bask,
And hear the blithesome vintage-strain
    Rise round the merry autumn task—
Shall I e'er see thy red must foam
    And seethe around thy peasants' limbs,
And hear, in many a cottage home,
    The children chant the vintage hymns—
Shall I e'er see one kind old man,
    Who, standing at the farm-yard gate,
Scarce paused the wanderer's face to scan,
    E'er spread the napkin, laid the plate
For simple feast of chestnuts boiled,
    And wine, whose grapes grew on the slope;
But to the traveller who had toiled,
    Three hours up hill a kaiser's tope:
Shall I hear his shrewd speech, and wise,
    Aim those swift shafts of native wit,
And mark each arrow as it flies,
    Strike home on sturdy wing, and hit?

"Why, sir, he sold us just like sheep,
  Though we, right willing to be sold,
Went gladly from his sordid keep
  To France's rich imperial fold."
Thus a few words, and shrewd compress'd,
  The story of King Victor's sale,
And the Savoyard but express'd
  All Europe's reading of the tale.
Shall I with Rousseau's volumes track
  Each road he has made haunted clay,
And echo his life's anthem back,
  "Fair Freedom does whole worlds outweigh?"
And so, perchance, my hero thought
  The Horace of the Georgian age;
Such echoes still to us are brought
  From many a brilliant witty page.
"Trust me," he writes, "that if I fall
  From greatness, grandeur, or from ease,
I shall not grieve, long sick of all
  The frigid pomps that worldlings please.
For me fair freedom and the choice
  Of friends, not Fashion's dolls, but men,
Whose heart I hear speak in their voice,
  And answer with my heart again."
So wrote he in that anxious hour,
  When foes assailed his father's name,
When waned the glorious statesman's power,
  And dulled the star of his great fame;

But grandly rose that brave old man,
    And with a bridegroom's gallant boast,
Glanced scorn from eyes that in their scan,
    Like lightnings scathed the opposing host ;
Then calmly turning from the rout
    Of those who shouted for his fall,
The haven of his youth sought out,
    The glades and groves of Houghton Hall.

CANTO III.

HOUGHTON HALL.

"Seen him I have, but in his happier hour
Of social pleasure ill exchanged for power—
Seen him, uncumbered with the venal tribe,
Smile without art, and win without a bribe."

POPE.

"These were the lively eyes and rosy hue
Of Robin's face, when Robin first I knew ;
The gay companion and the favourite guest,
Loved without awe, and without views caressed.
His cheerful smile and honest, open look
Added new graces to the truths he spoke ;
Then every man found something to commend,
The pleasant neighbour and the worthy friend."

LADY MARY WORTLEY MONTAGUE.

I.

But Houghton stood another fane
From the young bridegroom's happy home,
Reared high its state o'er Norfolk plain,
And stored the arts of Greece and Rome,
'Midst thicker groves and ampler seas
Of verdure, whose soft-wooded swell

D 2

Surged on its ocean-tide of trees,
　　That with the champaign rose and fell—
Rose the new hall and reared its crest,
　　And flowered into perfect form,
The haven where his bark found rest
　　And shelter from the threatened storm.
Old Norfolk Walpoles each would gaze
　　With wonder, could their eyes behold
The pomp, the splendours that now blaze
　　Where their plain manor stood of old,
For Italy was sacked to send
　　Her marbles to the stately walls,
And Persia's looms their colours blend,
　　Where the mute footstep sinking falls;
Around the gardens spread their state,
　　And seemed a theft from Eastern tales,
Of splendours that on caliphs wait,
　　And scents that spice the Orient gales;
Within the priceless canvas told
　　Its gorgeous tale of wealth and taste,
And Titian's purple, Guido's gold,
　　And Rubens' wanton roses' waste
Were flung imperially around
　　Upon Carrara's snowy field,
Till many a rood of marble ground
　　Those gorgeous colours had concealed;
And Vandyke lent his stately grace,
　　And Kneller gave his firm repose,

And Snyders from each market-place
    Purloined the choicest fruit that grows;
Here Bedford and here Chandos sent
    Some gem, their glorious galleries' pride—
Here pearl of Portland's softly blent
    Its lustre by Maratti's side;
And Florence, from her princes' wreck,
    Stript many a wall of richest worth;
And beauty came at Walpole's beck
    From many a rood of Roman earth,
And all that art and wealth could give,
    The brighter glowed beneath his eyes;
And all these glories seemed to live,
    As sentient he was there to prize.
The great, good man of ample heart,
    The sweetest temper of his age;
No arrow rankled there to smart,
    Nor wrong was treasured to enrage.
The beauty and the grace that shone
    Round Walpole in his bridal prime,
To his last years by him were worn,
    Though shadowed not effaced by time;
And to this world of living art—
    This glow, this glory, and perfume,
Comes Horace, bringing brain and heart,
    All vivid with his travels' bloom;
There revels he 'mid all that flush
    Of beauty, time had touched to mellow,

While down Life's stream, with brilliant rush,
　　Fly years none others ever fellow;
When, boyhood's doubts and fears dispelled,
　　The warmer sun of manhood rises,
And misty clouds the dawning held,
　　Are changed to Phœbus' golden friezes;
There met the brilliant throng at night,
　　Where Houghton's lord was Liber's priest,
And rolling hours of loud delight,
　　Hailed Bacchus guardian of the feast;
Scarce blither on Sicilian sod,
　　Around his chariot swelled the song,
Than those they chanted to the god
　　When Walpole led the strain along,
When crystal cups were brimming bright,
　　And beaded with the crimson wine,
And laughter led the hours of night,
　　In riot to Aurora's shrine;
But harmless riot, such as might
　　Win prudence to a passing smile;
Not that fierce flame athwart the night,
　　From Medmenham's dishonoured pile;
Not Le Despencer's rabble rout
　　Were those who met round Orford's board,
Nor theirs such orgies as rang out
　　When altar wine for ape was poured.
No—harmless the light arrows hit,
　　His humour shot in careless play,

And harmless shone his lambent wit,
  As lightnings on the first of May;
There satire lost her bitter sting,
  And wore the merry mask of joke;
There fancy flew on brilliant wing,
  And jovial staves like these awoke:

Lift the purple, lift the ruby,
  Lift the golden goblets high,—
Glow the warm Hispanian amber,
  Blush the blood of Burgundy.

Let each toper praise the drinking
  That he deemeth most divine,
Or the brave Burgundian vintage,
  Or the sunny Spanish wine.

This is golden as the flowing
  Of Pactolus 'neath the sun;
This is red as life-blood going
  From the warrior who has won.

By the topaz place the ruby,
  Each will praise his favourite stone;
Blush the red rose by the yellow,
  Each will pluck the one alone.

Tastes will differ, let us own it,
  And the crimson claret-chooser
Of the Lusitanian vintage,
  Be a resolute refuser.

Tastes will differ, who shall force you
  To disown your darling berry;
Who, by censure, shall divorce you
  From your love of port or sherry?

We are diverse in our drinking,
  But in adoration one,
Of the vine-crowned god, who sitteth
  Striding on full-bellied tun.

Hail to thee, O hail, Silenus,
  See each swing the green-leav'd thyrsus—
See each greet thee "Bacchi plenus,"
  With crowned cup and Bacchante verses.

II.

As the rich central diamond darks
  Each clustering ruby's reddest rays,
And seems to feed upon its sparks,
  And draw them to its brighter blaze;

So, 'midst the wits that flashed around,
    Shone Orford, with that ruling grace
That gave to licence fitting bound,
    To decency her proper place.
How well one sketched in pleasant whim—
    How well her graceful pencil drew
The portrait she had skill to limn,
    And boldness to hold up to view.
In days when friends grew cold or shy,
    Beat Wortley's heart with warmer glow;
The world his friend, she might decry,
    But praise him when it grew his foe.
Bright Wortley, in thy verse lives still
    The " Robin " of thy genial sketch—
The " Robin " whose majestic will,
    All epochs since have failed to match ;
Not Fox, nor Gray, nor Pitt, nor Peel,
    So felt the pulses of the land,
Knew when to crush with iron heel,
    And when caress with soothing hand ;
- But failed they more to match his heart—
    His honest heart set in his smile,
Whose goodness was its only art,
    Whose easiness his only guile ;
No statesman since could ever gain
    So brilliant and so true a verse,
Nor even Fox deserve the strain
    She flung upon thy glorious hearse ;

Though many a canvas holds imprest,
  The sturdy form, the rosy face,
'Tis Wortley's verse that mirrors best
  The lineaments we love to trace.
How pleasant, too, the task to turn
  From Pope's black rhyme at Hervey thrown,
To where, round Walpole's funeral urn,
  Hang verses he may proudly own.
Ah! well might grief of guest and friend
  In widening circles spread afar,
And England mourn, from end to end,
  The setting of her proudest star;
But not for him the knell was tolled,
  Where sleep the cherished of the land,
No anthem's thunder o'er him rolled,
  Grand welcome to their solemn band.
He willed to sleep beneath the soil
  His boyhood's steps so oft had trod,
Where near his grave his peasants toil,
  Or resting, rest beneath its sod—
Where he had seen his father laid—
  Where he had brought his happy bride—
Where waved the trees their friendly shade
  O'er the wide acres long his pride.
There came in after years that son,
  Who most upheld his father's fame,
Though in a gentler field he won
  The blazon that surrounds his name—

There Horace stood in bitter grief
  Beside his house's splendid wreck,
And saw the springtide bring its leaf,
  Neglected glade and grove to deck—
There poured his soul its sorrow forth,
  Lamenting over Houghton's fall,
Recalling sadly all the worth
  Of him who reared the stately hall.

HORACE WALPOLE TO GEORGE MONTAGUE.

Oh! my friend of school and college, let me pour my
  grief before you,
From my childhood's silent chambers, take my aching
  heart's lament;
It, maybe, in some future hour, should a grief like mine
  come o'er you,
I shall send you back the solace you will joy to feel
  you sent.

For, my friend, my heart is lonely, wan, and drooping
  unto madness,
And a waste is all around me in my childhood's happy
  home,

And a faintness falls upon me as I taste the springtide's
 sadness,
  In the happy glades and gardens where my boyhood
  used to roam.

For the springtide bringeth pleasure to the happy heart
 of childhood,
  Beating gladly as it greeteth the first primrose in the
  grass;
And the village maid bound homeward, as she trippeth
 through the wildwood,
  Loves the lengthening eves around her on the lone-
  ways she must pass.

And the spring moon peereth softly through the
 orchard's crimson blossoms,
  Where the stealing steps of lovers meet around the
  trysting tree;
And the luring light discloses not the deep abyss's
 chasms,
  And his manly form before her, she would risk them,
  could she see.

For the maid's heart melteth softly at such meeting in
 the gloaming,
  And her spirit sinketh helpless 'neath her lover's
  bounding arm ;

She will willing risk the future—all the grief and wrong
   swift coming,
And will yield another victim to a lover's luring
   charm.

When the spring has turned its blossoms to the ripe and
   golden apples,
   Languid stepping, wan and weary, she will seek
      again that tree,
When September's sun in setting all the hill with
   shadow dapples,
   Plucking autumn's fruit of sorrow from her spring-
      tide's bud of glee.

Still, to bud, and bird, and insect, and to loving youth
   and maiden,
   Comes the spring to wake to gladness all the pulses
      of their life,
Bird and insect chirp their carol, buds the heavy
   hedgerows laden,
   And to Will. and Susan courting, all the earth's with
      rapture rife.

But to me the springtide's coming brings no freshness
   on its breezes,
   And I wish its blossoms falling were to fall above my
      grave ;

Better I were lying silent, than to hear yon' bell, that
 freezes
  All my life-blood, knelling solemn over her I could
   not save.

Where yon turret cuts the elm-trees, there my mother,
 softly sleeping,
  Cannot hear me rave and call upon her cherished
   name in vain—
Cannot hear the downward falling of my tears, like
 raindrops weeping—
  Cannot breathe a word of solace to my heart's un-
   dying pain.

There my father slumbers soundly after all his life's
 long fever,
  'Scaped from enemies that hated, and from false
   friends that betrayed;
Freed at last from foe and traitor, from the spy and
 the deceiver,
  In the soil that knew his childhood are his glorious
   relics laid.

And what now for me remaineth, now my sun of life
 goes downward,
  But to say farewell for ever to the scenes of such deep
   sorrow,

And the wreck of Houghton quitting, swift to bend
  my passage townward;
  There to seek, if not a happy, yet a brighter-coloured
  morrow.

I will seek for some forgetting 'midst the busy life of
  London,
  Far from Houghton's graves and ruins, I will oil
  Life's chariot wheels;
Down the brilliant social groovings, from the dawn
  until the sun-down
  I will chase the siren Pleasure, as she rings her
  merry peals.

Where the lamps are shining brightly, and the curtains
  hide the dawning—
  Where the dice are loudly rattled, and the wine flows
  in the cup—
Where the hours, gaily gliding from the midnight to
  the morning,
  See the gamblers madly gamble, and the painted
  women sup.

There some pleasures still await me—there some solace
  shall console—
  There the darkness of my anguish may in drink
  dissolve away—

There my misery may be melted, like the pearl within
the bowl,
And my sorrows, with my guineas, be dissolved in
reckless play.

Nay, what madness working in my brain impels such
fevered longing;
Help me, friend, to lay the spirit, like a demon that
arises—
Help me banish these fierce fancies, now around me
thickly thronging—
Help me, Heaven, standing lonely, to do battle with
this crisis.

'Tis through such throes that most must pass,
  Some happy ones to that repose,
Which, facing calmly Memory's glass,
  Sees Sorrow bloom to Victory's rose,
Of conquests won, of duty done—
  Of vices vanquished, lusts down-trod,
Made stepping-stones, on which the man
  Mounts o'er his passions to his God ;
While some, for heaven's choice less framed,
  For the world's use more fit, perchance,
Creep from the warfare, somewhat maimed,
  And fling away the shattered lance
Of high resolve, that bore no deed
  Like those who sprang at morn to arms,

For Carthage's dear sake to bleed,
  And fall at eve 'neath Capua's charms:
So fails the heart in duty's cause,
  When sorrows draw their dark array ;
Should pleasure only give it laws,
  Its forces break and melt away ;
Then must we rank with those who turn
  From that tough fight our hero's name,
Content to see a classic urn,
  Or Gothic archway shrine his fame—
Content to feel that he, at least,
  If not a saint, was no great sinner ;
Just one of those to grace a feast,
  And be the hero of a dinner—
Just one to chain us by his wit,
  With charming ease become our debtor ;
Then deem us paid, himself well quit
  By sending us a graceful letter.
No; in Fame's Libro d'Oro we
  For Walpole claim a higher place,
Though its first pages sacred be
  To those who ran the martyr's race ;
Yet his not last in that array
  Of men who worked the world some good,
And, 'midst their epoch's coarser clay,
  Lived as their finer natures should.

E

Henceforth, we track him through those years
On which a happier era dawns,
And, faintly outlined, Strawberry rears
Her turrets 'midst the Twickenham lawns.

CANTO IV.

STRAWBERRY HILL.

——— ———

" Some talk of Gunnersbury,
    For Sion some declare,
And some say that with Chiswick House
    No villa can compare ;
But all the beaux of Middlesex,
    Who know the country well,
Say that Strawberry Hill, that Strawberry
    Doth bear away the bell.

" Though Surrey boast its Oatlands,
    And Claremont keeps so jim,
And though they talk of Southcotes,
    'Tis but a dainty whim !
For ask the gallant Bristow,
    Who does in taste excel,
If Strawberry Hill, if Strawberry
    Don't bear away the bell."
                    EARL OF BATH.

————— ———

ALAS ! as I approach the theme
    I'd fain my rhyme should nobly grace,
I feel 'twas but an idle dream
    That I could fitly paint the place ;

E 2

The subject tempts, and I draw near,
  Then shiver on its very edge,
As a child pauses, dumb with fear,
  Upon the land's last shelving ledge,
While on his gaze an ocean swells,
  And threatening billows forward throws;
Or, like the diver Browning tells,
  A beggar plunged, an emperor rose;
But could I hope such happy leap,
  Despite the raging ocean's whirl,
Proud would I feel to dare the deep,
  But prouder still to pluck the pearl—
That pearl, the theme that I would grace,
  However poorly, with my verse;
To fit it for its destined place
  Amid the thousand gems of hers—
Of her, the queen whom Strawberry thrones—
  Amid its gardens, lawns, and meads,
Which Thames, with silver girdle zones,
  Where charm to sister charm succeeds.

To Richmond summer comes, as queen
  To sister queen with regal air,
And finds her throned, and with the mien
  Of one who has the right to wear
The stately grace of queenly birth,
  " Born in the purple " flower crowned,
Anointed beauty of the earth,

And through the ages, world renowned—
Our English Imogen, to whom
    All other creatures give their best,
The grace of grace, the bloom of bloom,
    Are hers Earth's darling long contest ;
There April steps knee-deep in flowers—
    There comes the May, a gorgeous giver—
There June sees, through long golden hours,
    Her sunshine on the happy river ;
From day to day, and week to week,
    The summer ocean richer sprays
Foams roses, fit for Beauty's cheek,
    And flowers all the wooded ways ;
Its billows surge mile after mile,
    Mile after mile in lavish sweep,
And grandly lift afar the pile
    Of lordly Windsor's tower and keep ;
To them fair Surrey freely sends
    Her pastures gold, her gardens' bloom ;
Where all the flushing landscape blends
    Its glowing threads on Flora's loom :
There sweeps bright Ceres' golden tide
    In richer floods than Neptune owns,
And breaks in rapture on the side
    Of the soft height that Richmond thrones,
And leaps o'er all the hills' ascent,
    And tosses up that glorious park,
With crimson mist of May besprent,

And chestnuts lighting all the dark
Recesses of their glooming boughs,
   With twice ten thousand tapers' blaze,
And glades a sheet of hawthorn snows,
   Far flashing through the summer's haze,
Where all this lavish ocean's swell
   Finds form and grace in gardens trim,
Rise, Strawberry, rise, and bear the bell—
   The world's unrivalled Gothic whim.

What haunted airs around thee blow,
   Fair Strawberry, from the ancient years—
What roses of old legends grow,
   Thick clustered, as the traveller nears
Thy front, for as he steps they spring,
   Making the place an Arthur land,
Enwrought with idylls of a king,
   And tales of his romantic band;
For here a king has left his fame,
   The monarch of twelve acres' tract—
King Horace was our monarch's name,
   And Strawberry his title backed;
Then Twickenham rose thy meads to note,
   Then thy fair banks in favour grew,
And on thy river barge and boat
   The fair, the wise, the witty drew.
The castle of thy monarch rose,
   As from some Gothic fairy's hand,

Till over Thames its shadow throws
The loveliest villa in the land;
There reigned King Horace in his state,
While round him clustered, one by one,
Fair mansions of the rich and great,
All turning to their central sun ;
There Pope his rival villa plants,
And pours his suit in Wortley's ear,
While she laughs louder than he rants,
And stabs him with a bitter jeer ;
There Gay, protected by his Duchess,
Dares to encounter "Lockett's" son,
And writes immortal fables, such as
Beat all that La Fontaine has done—
There stately, 'midst its elm-tree walks,
A gun-shot off, stands famous Ham—
There Thames, when "Pryor's Kitty" talks,
Grows classic as another Cam—
There Clive, stage laurels well resigned,
Lives happier 'midst her laurel groves,
While, near her, Horace joys to find
The friend of early days and loves,
For Howard here had pitched her tent,
Ruling her little circle still,
And all Horatio's subjects bent
Before the Queen of Marble Hill—
Here reigned those two old friends and true,
Recalling many a scandal past,

Exchanging *cancans, billets-doux,*
    Gay, pleasant, witty to the last ;
This was a pleasant life, at least,
    The sternest moralist must own him,
Happy amid that landscape's feast,
    And where such willing subjects throne him ;
Still something seem to lack his walls,
    And incomplete his home reposes,
Till three fair faces light his halls,
    And three bright rosebuds bloom to roses ;
Strange story linked to these bright girls,
    That old romance which all have read,
O'er which have drooped the maiden's curls—
    O'er which the maiden's heart has bled.

EDWARD WALPOLE AND MARY CLEMENTS.

How sweet the tales of love they wove,
    Where rank unequal was no bar,
Where she bent o'er her knight to love,
    And he looked up as to a star—

The grand old times when hardihood,
    The lion heart, the handsome face
Softened the damsel's sternest mood,
    And won her to a willing grace.

Then, regal in her queenly state,
    The lady raised him to her side,
Henceforth to walk with her elate,
    Proud bridegroom of a peerless bride.

Far other is this tale of mine;
    Here all the pride of rank is his,
His mien to her is all divine,
    She has her love and only this.

He looks the June's imperious lord,
    She seems the May-tide's gentle queen;
Her realm a strip of village sward,
    His on Olympus should have been.

She loves him as the rose the June,
    And turns to sun her in his eyes,
Unwitting that she loves too soon,
    And too intensely for disguise.

Laid at his feet is all her pride,
    Her woman's crown is in the dust;
She scarce dare ask to be his bride,
    She only feels that love she must.

He ardent pleads, she strives to speak,
    Her hand is raised to hide the glow
That mantles through it o'er her cheek,
    As rose's red on rose's snow.

Gently he plucked that village rose,
　　And bore it to his stately home;
His tenderest care henceforth she knows,
　　And never asks from it to roam.

And yet, perchance, some grief there preyed
　　Upon her loving woman's heart—
Perchance upon her spirit weighed
　　A sorrow, though unowned its smart.

For she ne'er won the sweetest word
　　From manly lips in woman's ears;
"My own" oft whispered, still unheard,
　　"My wife" through all those patient years.

Sadly her eyes strained towards the time,
　　But never came that honeymoon;
So ruffled ran her girlhood's rhyme,
　　So jangled all her life's sad tune.

Then three fair girls around her bloomed,
　　And ripened into richest grace;
She felt she had their beauty doomed,
　　And saw her sin in each fair face.

And when the son, who should have been
　　His father's heir, his mother's joy,
Was born, she looked with anguish keen
　　On him, her lovely landless boy.

Swiftly she faded from the earth,
　Poor victim to the world's wise laws,
That wage their war with woman's worth,
　And ever crush a woman's cause.

Who o'er the wild scarce trodden paths
　Of some deserted garden goes,
Oft finds amidst the matted swathes,
　And lost to view the fairest rose.
So grew neglected from their birth,
　Those three who should by right of grace
Have regnant reigned o'er that proud earth,
　Where Beauty holds her chosen place;
But exiles they from that charm'd ground,
　Trod by a few fair favoured feet—
Legitimacy sternly frowned,
　Though owning nothing half so sweet;
Perchance, for that her jealous ban
　Lay heavier over each fair head,
And hoped to interdict the man
　Who thought outside her pale to wed.
What! wed a girl whose only charms
　Were in her temper, heart, and face;
Fashion her cohorts called to arms,
　Decorum blushed at the disgrace;
Stiff Etiquette in fright half rose,
　Infringing on her own stern laws,
That one might sit until she froze,
　But never start, whate'er the cause.

Sad had it been for these sweet helots,
　　Had women only had their way,
For where, alas! such bitter zealots
　　As these fair bits of fashion's clay?
But man, more generous, threw his shield
　　Chivalric o'er each lovely form;
And Strawberry gave a sunny field
　　And shelter from the world's loud storm.
Henceforth the Gothic halls grew bright
　　When these "slight slips of girlhood" went
And flushed each chamber with the light
　　Of their young spirits' glad content.
And soon the rosebuds that one twined
　　With whiter fingers round her brow,
For statelier fillet were resigned,
　　When pearls and ermine wreathed its snow;
A little while the pearls fell down,
　　For croix patté and flower-de-luce,
As standing near his brother's throne,
　　Duke Gloucester crowned the fair recluse.
Bright Waldegrave, how thy lovely face,
　　From Reynolds' canvas shineth yet,
How Ramsay's pencil loved to trace
　　The features none who see forget!
Of those who rose to such fair state,
　　And shine across a hundred years,
Bright stars that none to-day can mate,
　　Sisters whom none but sister peers.

A DAY AT STRAWBERRY HILL.

(*Time about* 1755.)

The day half spent to those poor wights,
  Who rise with rise of sun,
To Strawberry's Lord and his gay clique,
  Seems only now begun.

The beauties still their gossip hold,
  While frothing from the mill,
The chocolate brims those dainty cups,
  Where Watteau's groups live still.

The tender Sèvres' glowing tints,
  And *Rose da Barry's* flush,
Melt round the rose of each fair hand,
  Blush wedded unto blush.

The simple morning garb folds round
  Each slender sister grace,
Unpowdered flows the golden hair,
  Unpatched the dimpled face.

It is the fairest hour of all,
  Their own especial one ;
Riot the roses in the morn,
  Look lilies to the sun.

What whiter lily can he see
  Rise on its slender stem ;
What red do any roses own
  That is not matched in them?

What silver chime of bells can peal,
  So sweet as their sweet laughter;
That running round might fetch a soul
  From every beam and rafter?

At times its merry notes ring out,
  Like joy-bells to his heart;
Then swifter runs his gliding pen,
  And brighter glows his art,

Who, sitting in his study's calm,
  His pleasant labour plies,
While clocks chime on, and morn to noon,
  And noon to even flies.

From the stained window o'er his head,
  A ray of topaz streams ;
And as he writes, the richer ray
  Of Fancy's topaz gleams.

The crimson roses' glutting glow
  Rains redly from the pane ;
Romance's rose springs redder far,
  That blooms from heart and brain.

O happy toil of lettered ease,
   In study's cloister still ;
O happy author, who may write
   Or pause at Fancy's will !

Who sees the visions of his brain,
   Thick flowering o'er his page,
And from the present wanders free,
   Through all the Gothic age.

Where old Otranto's helmet dim,
   Waves dreamily its plume;
And all in vague mysterious haze,
   Drifts dark through Gothic gloom.

And thus for him his fancies weave
   A curtain's purple fold,
That fences round his small demesne,
   From the world's outer cold.

The day glides on ; each sister now
   Puts on her charms' whole armour ;
The patch and powder contrast give,
   Nor touch of red will harm her.

And now from closet comes the Lord
   Of Strawberry's demesne ;
And boat and barge and coach bring down
   Half London's courtly train.

Brilliant the groups that cluster now
    Upon the close-cut sward;
St. James's sends its brightest belles,
    And Twickenham sends her bard.

Here Selwyn walks like life in death,
    With face of livid hue;
Here Riot sees her favourite child
    In March not yet "old Q."

Here Lady Suffolk grown a prude,
    And pattern for the age,
On Clive and Pritchard looks askance,
    Half dubious of the stage.

And now there buzzes from the throng
    A murmur, half applause,
As, with his courtly air, the host
    Leads in the lovely cause.

'Tis Gunning's self, half arch, half shy,
    Half come in masquerade,
So quaint, so charming, is the garb
    She calls to fashion's aid.

'Tis Psyche's self in Gunning's guise,
    For hovering o'er her head
Is Psyche's brilliant butterfly,
    Its joyous pinions spread.

And lappets crossed beneath the chin,
  And ribbons pink and green,
And thousand coquetries of art
  Proclaim her Beauty's queen.

Gaily they scatter o'er the grounds,
  Search all within their reach ;
And here they praise a tulip-bed,
  And there they pluck a peach.

Now Pope's last verses slyly quote,
  Now wail Clarissa's woes,
Now Lady Hervey's house discuss,
  And what her birth-day clothes.

Now lifts the moon her pearly globe
  Through evening's purple haze ;
The river tempts to Twickenham Ait,
  And Hesper lends his blaze.

The parties formed with laughter all
  In boat and barge embark ;
Some vote for Ham's sequestered groves,
  And some for Richmond Park.

Thus ran the three fair Walpoles' days,
  With none to chide or carp,
With beauty for life's glittering woof,
  And happiness its warp.

Away they glide, those glittering years,
  Till each fair sister made a wife,
And ranked amid her father's peers,
  Sheds grace upon the matron's life.
Perchance to-day some poet's heart,
  He gazing, aches with sudden pain
Before a picture, forming part
  Of the rich bloom of Reynolds' reign ;
A sweet fair face, an English face,
  With pensive eyes—soft homes of love,
And that mild, tender woman's grace
  That nothing emblems like the dove.
This is Maria, she who wed
  Beneath the shadow of the throne,
Though here for crown around her head,
  Shines aureole of love alone ;
And near her hangs the rarest gem,
  Of all Sir Joshua's diamond mine,
Where, in the grace bequeathed to them,
  Maria's matchless daughters shine.
And gazing on these portraits now,
  This world of ours seems cold and bare ;
Faint on the century's shadowed brow,
  Shine stars we deem the brightest there.

Old house! how often through thy rooms
    Have swept those beauteous three,
Who glow on Reynolds' canvas yet
    In all that witchery.

Of high-bred mien, and arch sweet smile,
    Which steal the heart away;
E'er 'gainst the magic of the smile,
    It has found time to pray.

O beauteous sisters, painted there,
    With all the artist's grace!
Well—well it is there comes not life
    To warm each lovely face.

For e'en in gazing on them now,
    The gazer's heart will ache;
He looks and longs that they may live,
    And he die for their sake.

And have thy walls indeed looked on
    Those lovely sisters three?
Old house, whose front from out thy grove,
    Now looketh forth on me.

And hast thou seen them full of life,
    Come gliding in at morn,
While as they passed a richer day,
    A fuller sun seemed born?

Hast seen the peach-bloom ripen fast,
    On each transparent cheek;
Wax richer tints from day to day,
    Then fade from week to week?

Ah! was it so? Ah, then, old house,
    I may not envy thee;
I may not wish all thou hast seen,
    That I, too, were to see.

For from the canvas ever beams
    The same bewitching smile;
The years glide on, but they with them
    Nor fade nor age the while.

One ever o'er the tambour-frame,
    The same slight figure bends;
And on each softly-rounded cheek,
    White rose with crimson blends.

They take the same sweet counsel still,
    O'er that old walnut-table;
Repeat the same light gossip, tell
    Who's wed, and who in sable.

The old-world grace and old-world garb
 Each graceful figure fold ;
'Tis only on the canvas that
 The fashion grows not old.

I see them still, old house, as thou
 Hast seen them years ago,
When through thy perfumed chambers swept
 Their garments' gracious flow.

Then keep thy stories of the past,
 Of beauty that is fled ;
Of belle and beau, and courtier, now
 Long numbered with the dead.

I do not wish to read the tale
 Thou hoardest on thy gloom ;
Of rose of beauty fading fast,
 And sinking to the tomb.

I turn from all thou canst unfold,
 To praise the artist's skill,
Upon whose canvas lives for me
 Each blooming beauty still.

O, artist of the tender soul,
 And of the courtly hand,
Who painted well for many a year
 The loveliest of the land,

There never sat before thy brush,
   Three of more perfect grace;
As rosebud matched with rosebud seems,
   So is each beauteous face.

Hang ever 'neath that ancient roof,
   Smile ever on its gloom;
Smile ever on its chambers sweet,
   With rose-leaves past their bloom.

The same sweet faces that have smiled
   At Lady Mary's wit,
In days when Walpole gossiped of
   The rising star of Pitt.

Methinks I see through mist of years,
   Those faultless features take
A terror from the volume first
   Read for the author's sake.

But as the story deepened, still
   Read on with pale affright,
That sent the helmet's shivering plume,
   Through all their dreams that night.

Quaint house, I could for ever dream
   On all thy antique lore;
But stream and time alike glide by,
   As I rest on the oar.

Farewell awhile the olden dream,
    Farewell the good old days !
And let me think the present holds
    Some virtue and some praise.

I pause while yet the golden sands
    Run sparkling from the glass ;
While yet the chime of merry hours,
    Scarce minds men how they pass.
While yet the sun is in the sky,
    The dew upon the flower ;
And still it is life's carnival,
    And still its noontide hour.
While yet that galaxy of gems,
    Shines in the epochs setting,
And none thinks time can dim its light,
    And none dreams of forgetting.
While Gunning's star is in its prime,
    And Wortley's not yet paling ;
And courtiers' eyes the rising orb
    Of young Prince George are hailing.
This was a time of ampler range,
    Of livelier tone and colour ;
Of shape and fashion nobler far,
    Of wit and humour fuller
Than these dull days on which our lot
    (Or do we merit better?)

Has fallen, catching sparks of wit
   From some Walpolian letter.
He wrote reflecting on its page,
   The hours' light life around him,
And who his morning visitors,
   And where the evening found him.
We warm us in these rays of wit,
   That from that era shine ;
We read those letters o'er and o'er,
   And deem them half divine.
We ponder o'er their brilliant tales,
   Re-coin their witty stories,
And strutting in their brilliant plumes,
   To-day's poor jackdaw glories.
And thus I seek to steal a spark
   Of those bright times transmitting,
To catch a gleam of Reynolds' age,
   Rich days and colours flitting.
The impress of a bygone day,
   By Beauty's tone pervaded ;
To fasten on my page, e'er yet
   Its memory all has faded.
For still there live, 'midst us to-day,
   A few— a favoured few—
Who saw the last bright sunset ray,
   That age in setting threw.
Still Guizot lives, and Houghton writes,
   To tell us of the two

Fair sisters, who in their young prime
　　Burke, Hastings, Walpole knew.
Some dozen more, perchance, recall
　　The tones of Mary Berry ;
The accents that waged witty war
　　With Charlie Fox and Sherry.
Ask these if with her faded not
　　All save what memories shrine
Of the old days, whose cup was brimmed
　　With wit pure as its wine.
Ask these if aught we boast to-day
　　Can mirror back the grace
Of the bright girls whose beauty's dawn
　　Sir Joshua loved to trace.
The famous clubs are silent now,
　　Fled is their brilliant era,
And Selwyn's ghost might wander through
　　Them all and never hear a
Bon-mot worth his while repeating,
　　A *cancan* or a story
Like those that rattled through the room
　　When White's was in its glory.
The diners-out a dismal set,
　　Now Moore, Smith, Hook are dead,
Talk feeble scandal round the boards,
　　Whence port and plate have fled,
And sipping *Chateau Margaux*, prate,
　　Amid the fruit and flowers,

The wretched slang, replacing now
    The wit of those dead hours.
The women, where the peach-like bloom,
    And where the high-bred grace;
The softness of the melting eye,
    The faultlessness of face
All fled? Nay, scarcely so, while yet
    Fair Strawberry's turrets rise,
And Waldegrave gathers 'neath her roof
    The witty and the wise.
To that charmed focus still the rays
    Of choicest minds converge;
And wit reviving lives by Thames,
    While London sings its dirge.

A MESSAGE.

Who may I dare to hope from time
    Will snatch one idle hour
    To search if, haply, any flower
Bloom 'mid these weeds of rhyme?

Not she to whom I vow my lay—
    Engirt with queenly state,
    On whom a hundred poets wait,
She has no time to stay.

A thousand claims around her press,
   A thousand voices call,
   Were she to pause or list to all
Who crave her smile to bless

The glad triumphant march, I ween,
   Of her life's brilliant pageant
   Would cease, and ball-rooms lack the radiant
Appearing of their queen.

Not kindred who stand near in blood,
   Or one or two of these ;
   For e'en true poets fail to please
All of their cousinhood.

True poets e'en lack their reward—
   They are the first to sneer.
   'Tis rarely author's lot to hear
One gentle, kindly word

From those from whom in ardent youth
   He thought to catch a ray
   Of light, or hear a kind voice say,
" This is well done, in sooth."

But coldest critic's coldest mood
   Will give more generous meed,
   Nor ever make the young heart bleed
As those placed near in blood.

From strangers can I hope to gain
  A gentle thought or smile,
  That may in failure's hour beguile
My heart of half its pain?

Nay, they can walk in garden ways,
  And gather from the boughs
  Down-drooping blossoms rich as those
From Tennysonian sprays.

Then who will care to stretch a hand
  To gather these pale flowers,
  That budded in the winter hours,
And from a sterile land?

Yes, one I know, one student friend,
  Who, 'midst his college lore,
  Will lovingly read o'er and o'er
The pages that I send.

Oft, while I wrote, I saw the halls
  Run grey round the quadrangle,
  And flowers, in every nook and angle,
Burn redly on the walls;

Saw the rich creeper's scarlet flames
  And bright geranium's blaze
  Light the grey walls with ruddy rays,
And fire the window-frames.

From one of which I oft, with him,
    Have watched the evening's close,
    When the June twilight's sweet repose
Stole round the cloisters dim.

And he, I know, from out my book
    Will see old faces spring,
    Recalling how the hours took wing
In that dim college nook ;

And, for their sake and mine, will prize
    The volume I now send,—
    A happy book, that goes, dear friend,
To meet thy sunny eyes,—

The eyes that mine so oft have met
    With loyal love and truth,
    That, though I live ten lives, in sooth,
I never shall forget.

NOTES TO "STRAWBERRY HILL."

—————

Page 1, line 1.

"*July's last eve, and William king,*
The century scarce eight months begun."

Robert (afterwards Sir Robert) Walpole was married to Catherine, daughter of John Shorter, Esq., of Bybrook, in Kent, on the 30th of July, 1700. They spent their honeymoon at Houghton Hall, which I suppose them to reach the following evening.

Page 4, line 16.

"*Who hall and boroughs, wealth and name.*"

Robert Walpole succeeded not only to the family property, but the family boroughs, and sat in the second short Parliament, which was called at the conclusion of the reign of William III.

Page 4, line 19.

"*Of those young years he freely gave,*
With their first-fruit of college hours."

Robert Walpole had been distinguished at Cambridge; but on the death of his two elder brothers resigned his scholarship, and threw aside sundry attempts at literary composition, and accompanied his father to Houghton, to go through what the old gentleman thought the proper career to render the youngster competent to succeed him with credit in the important position of a Norfolk squire."—Eliot Warburton's *Memoirs of Horace Walpole*, vol. i.

Page 6, line 19.

" The star of him men named the peer
Of Compton, Stanhope, Halifax."

In the first Parliament of Queen Anne, he became known to Spencer Compton, afterwards Earl of Wilmington ; James, afterwards Earl Stanhope, the Earl of Sunderland, and Lord Halifax. Even the Lord Treasurer, Godolphin, looked upon him as worthy of attention, and introduced him to the great man of his age, the famous Duke of Marlborough.—*Memoirs of H. Walpole*, vol. i.

Page 7, line 26.

" And waken fools from their sick dream."

It has become a kind of fashion of late years with a certain set of religionists, to speak with contempt of that great movement in the public mind which counteracted the insidious efforts of James II. to throw religious freedom back a couple of centuries.—*Ibid.*

Page 8, line 15.

" Came Marlborough with his glittering fame—
Came Walpole with his zeal unfeigned."

Undeterred by the fate of his friend, or the punishment he had already suffered, Walpole continued his opposition with increasing zeal, particularly insisting on the importance of the Protestant succession, and exposing the intrigues of the Pretender and his adherents.

Page 10, line 18.

" Two, deep in youth's delicious themes."

Among the numerous associates of his own age and rank, with whom he was most familiar, he distinguished three with a fervency of regard unusual even among schoolboys. The first and dearest of these juvenile friends was Thomas Gray.—*Ibid.*

Page 14, line 14.

" Come half the sages, all the wits,
And Swift is decent as in lawn."

In Mrs. Howard's circle, Pope became playful, and Swift decent.—*Ibid.*

Page 15, line 2.

" O'ertopt the fame of that Greek mount."

The names of the three Maries, Bellenden, Lepel, and Wortley Montague, were as famous in their day as those of the rival deities who competed on Mount Ida for the golden apple.—*Memoirs of H. Walpole.*

Page 15, line 16.

" The softness of a m ther's face,
That ceased to smile just as his part."

Lady Walpole died in August, 1737, at the very time when the son, to whom she had been so admirable a mother, promised by his talents and disposition to prove a source of the deepest gratification to her maternal heart. In another year he would have completed the course of study which was to fit him for obtaining a place in society such as should satisfy her hopes and ambition. But it was not to be. The fond mother sunk at the very threshold of her aspirations for her favourite child, and the sweet sympathies of her nature never more soothed and gladdened the heart of her son.— *Ibid.*

Page 15, line 19.

" And left that death-chill on his heart
No sun in life could warm again."

This was a heavy blow to the young student; an irreparable loss. All his affections were centred upon his mother. She was the sun of his domestic system; and, her light quenched, all to him was darkness.—*Ibid.*

Page 29, line 21.

" And, as he rose, beneath him lay
A house and vine, not famous yet."

It was in 1736 that Rousseau and Madame de Warens took possession of " Les Charmettes," and in 1739 that Horace Walpole and Gray were travelling through Savoy : so that they may have beheld from the heights above the house where dwelt this singular pair. In fact, however, Claude Anet died previously to Madame de Warens moving to Les Charmettes; but this anachronism may, I hope, meet with pardon.

Page 30, line 13.

" *And thou, dear youth, the young Anet,*
Whom Nature seemed to mark for fame."

Claude Anet was a peasant of Montru, whom Madame de Warens had taken into her service. There is but little said of him in Rousseau's Memoirs; but that little is so well said, that I can hardly fancy any one reading the description and not feeling its charm. It is the portrait of a young, simple, fervent nature entirely unspoiled by the world, with something of the true Arcadian flavour, and of an intellect which, had his life been spared, must have led him to distinction. " He became a real botanist," says Rousseau, " and, had he not died young, he had been famed in this science as much as he deserved to be as an honest man."

Page 31, line 5.

" *Within this little circle locked,*
Their wishes, cares, their hearts were one."

" Thus was established among us three a society without, perhaps, an example on earth. All our wishes, our cares, our hearts were one. None of them passed beyond this little circle. . . . . . That which prevented constraint among us was our extreme reciprocal confidence, and that which prevented dulness was our being always employed."—*Memoirs of J. J. Rousseau.*

Page 33, line 1.

" *Why, sir, he sold us just like sheep.*"

This and the three following lines are almost verbatim the observation made to the author by the Savoyard farmer, whose homely fare and mother wit he has sought to depict.

Page 34, line 2.

" *And with a bridegroom's gallant boast.*"

Sir Robert's position was one of great danger; though, as his son said, " He boasted like a bridegroom."—Eliot Warburton's *Memoirs.*

G

Page 56, line 15.

Edward Walpole.

Sir Robert Walpole's second son, Edward, whose appearance was
so much in his favour, that the Italian ladies gave him the name of
" the handsome Englishman."

Page 56, line 15.

Mary Clements.

When passing through the shop (over which he lodged), one of
the apprentices frequently attracted Walpole's notice. She was a
beautiful young woman, of the name of Mary Clements. Mr.
Walpole soon contrived to have frequent interviews with her, and
gave her many little presents, but not so secretly as to escape the
notice of her mistress, who sent for her father to take her away from
temptation into the country. Together they lectured her upon the
impropriety of receiving attentions from a gentleman, and endeavoured to convince her how much more it would be to her
advantage to be the wife of a respectable tradesman. These
representations appeared to produce due effect, and the girl left the
room apparently to prepare for her departure, but to them she never
returned. On leaving the room, where she had been forced to listen
to their remonstrances, she had rushed to the apartment of " the
handsome Englishman," and when he received her with open arms,
she vowed that she would never leave him, nor did she. Mr. Walpole was devoted to her, befriended all her family, and treated her
with respect and consideration, though he never married her.—*Ibid.*

Page 57, line 1.

" *Then regal in her queenly state,*
The lady raised him to her side."

From the universal recognition of the dignity of woman, and of
their moral superiority over their knights, was devised another
rule, by which the homage of a knight of inferior, and even very
inferior rank to her own, was quite allowable to a lady of high
birth. But the chivalrous code denied her the homage of a baron
of higher degree, for fear she might be less exacting and imperious
with one whose rank imposed some consideration.—*History of
Chivalry.*

Page 58, line 17.

" *Then three fair girls around her bloomed.*"

These were three girls, who, as they grew up towards womanhood, threatened to eclipse the renown of the beautiful Gunnings.
—*Memoirs of Horace Walpole.*

Page 58, line 21.

" *And when the son who should have been.*"

The fourth child was a boy, and shortly after his birth, poor
erring devoted Mary Clements died. Deep was the grief of the
father of her children, and he mourned her loss as a fond husband
mourns the deprivation of the best of wives.—*Ibid.*

Page 60, line 15.

" *For statelier fillet were resigned.*"

Maria Walpole married first, James, 3rd Earl of Waldegrave, and
secondly, H.R.H. William Henry, Duke of Gloucester. Her sister,
Laura, married the Hon. and Rev. Frederick Keppel, son of the
Earl of Albemarle, and afterwards Bishop of Exeter. Charlotte
Walpole married Lord Huntingtower, eldest son of Lionel, 3rd
Earl of Dysart. These were the three daughters of poor Mary
Clements, the tailor's apprentice.

Page 60, line 21.

" *Bright Waldegrave, how thy lovely face*
From Reynolds' canvas smileth yet!"

The portraits of Laura and Charlotte were painted together by
Ramsay. Maria was painted by Sir Joshua Reynolds. The reader
must not confound the three daughters of Edward Walpole and
Mary Clements with the three beauties of a later generation, the
Ladies Waldegrave, who were the daughters of Maria Walpole by
her first marriage with Lord Waldegrave, and of course the grand-
daughters of Mary Clements.

Page 63, line 9.

" *Where old Otranto's helmet dim.*"

The " Castle of Otranto " was not published till 1764, so that I
must here again plead guilty to a, I trust, harmless anachronism.

Page 64, line 21.

" 'Tis Psyche's self in Gunning's guise."

Yesterday, after chapel, the duchess brought home Lady Coventry to feast me, and *a feast she was!* She is a fine figure, and vastly handsome. Her dress was a sort of black silk sack, made for a large hoop, which she wore without any, and it trailed a yard on the ground. She had on a cobweb laced handkerchief, a pink satin long cloak, lined with ermine mixed with squirrel skin. On her head a French cap, that just covered the top of her head of blond, and *stood in the form of a butterfly, with the wings not quite extended,* frilled sort of lappets, *crossed under her chin, and tied with pink and green ribbon,* a head-dress that would have charmed a shepherd!— *Autobiography of Mrs. Delany,* vol. iii. p. 300.

Page 67, line 1.

The three sisters.

The ladies Laura, Horatia, and Charlotte Waldegrave, daughters of James and Maria, Earl and Countess Waldegrave, painted by Sir Joshua Reynolds, and now the property of Frances, Countess of Waldegrave.

MISCELLANEOUS POEMS.

—·◆·◆·◆·——

THE SAILING OF THE "GOLDEN FLEECE,"

With the 73rd (Perthshire) Regiment on Board, from Queenstown,
November 24th, 1866.

Thou noble ship! no theme more meet for poet's verse
    to-day—
Ride o'er the seas in triumph, ride on thy gallant way ;
Ride on, thou classic vessel, with thy proud and golden
    name,
For England trusts to thee, to-day, the guardians of
    her fame ;
And with that glorious freightage, with the jewels of
    her pride,
Oh! ride thee on, triumphant, o'er the tempest and the
    tide.
See! see! them thronging on thy decks; see each
    young soldier's brow
Grow sadder as he gazes on the land receding now.
Oh! tears are rushing blindly into each young warrior's
    eyes,

Till the heart bursts all its barriers, and they flow
without disguise.
Weep, noble ones—weep freely; is there one in your
proud band
That would not weep to part from Old England's
cherished land?

And there are some whose hearts are rushing wildly
back, to-day,
To Scotland's dear and noble land, to her heather and
her brae;
And dim, thro' tears, on memory now, her purple
mountains rise,
The bonny Highland heather, and the glorious Scottish
skies;
But deeper cause for manly tears than native braes or
heather
Is the snapping of the links that have bound fond lives
together—
Is the thinking of some sister fair, of a comrade, or a
brother,
Of the sinking of a father's heart, of the anguish of a
mother—
Very sacred is your weeping, and great England
deemeth now
Such sons the proudest jewels she could wear upon her
brow;

And, watching fondly o'er you, such tears as these
   she'll hold
Dearer still than all her greatness, richer far than all
   her gold.
But not alone from noble hearts and gallant youths
   like these
Steals the muffled note of anguish on the chill November breeze;
There are rougher natures breaking down beneath the
   touch of grief,
There are hearts still strangers to the tears that bring
   their own relief;
To them nor hope nor memory brings a softening of
   their woe—
They but suffer, and are heart-sick, and that is all they
   know.
With pallid cheek, and teeth set firm, they stand there
   still and mute,
And some will deem them stolid, with the nature of the
   brute.
But God, it may be, looking down on those poor
   soldiers, knows
A grief to him as sacred as the others' softer woes.

Howe'er that be, oh! may He bless and guide ye on
   your way—
Farewell! mine own heart sinketh low to see ye sail
   to-day;

Like you, my heart is rushing back to other times and
skies ;
Like you, I see them dimly, for the hot tears in mine
eyes—
There, there, I can but bless you, and your captain,
and your ship,
As her sails swell to the breezes, and her timbers gladly
dip
Within the waves that bear her far and farther on her
track,
Till the English shores have faded from the eyes still
gazing back.
Farewell! God guide her safely over all her destined
way,
Who has our England's jewels in her keeping placed
to-day.

A LETTER FROM THE TROPICS.

Far from foggy skies of England, far from England's
cold and gloom,
Now my spirits rise elastic, now my heart to beat has
room.
All things are changed around me, all things are bright
and fair,
Oh, the radiant tropic climate ; oh, the blessed light and
air !

What has England ever given that I should care to
    part?
Scarce a hand I cared for grasping, scarce a warm or
    loving heart.
All my nature has been stifled by her raw and murky
    weather,
Where two golden days of summer scarce were seen to
    glow together.
Who would breathe the fog of England, who would
    gaze on her grey sky,
Who could bask away existence where these summer
    islands lie?
Well the *Golden Fleece* has speeded, happy those whom
    she has brought,
Happy I on whom her voyage such a glowing change
    has wrought;
Wish me joy, dear friends in England, wish me joy that
    I am here,
Where my heart has oped to rapture in the happy
    hemisphere.

Last night I lay upon the deck, I saw the Southern
    moon arise
Round her golden globe triumphant—mock the moon of
    English skies;
I saw the purple pavement break in flames around the
    ship,
And spray in golden sparkles round her timbers' rushing
    dip.

How balmy was the midnight air, that kissed my
    grateful brow ;
How strange to think of England plunged in her
    midwinter, now
Of snow, perchance, in London's streets, and ice upon
    her river,
Of burly forms in great coats wrapt, or ragged forms
    that shiver
At each keen blast that drives along, and bites the thin
    clad frame
Of women struck by Winter's hand, who perish in their
    shame,
Where, huddled 'neath some bridge's arch, they strove
    to fan life's flame.
How strange to feel that such things were, while all
    around me here
Glowed the summer of the world in the tropics'
    hemisphere !

See the ship sails swiftly onward, through the sunlit
    straits of Sunda ;
See each islet streak the ocean, each an ocean's Rosa
    Munda ;
Ocean's roses are these islets, Venus' baskets heaped
    with flowers,
Golden gleam the insects glancing, rain the leaves in
    roseate showers ;

Flash like jewels pinions spreading of the topaz-painted
birds,
All the languid air is murm'rous with the music of
strange words.
Oh, the beauteous bay of Angor! oh, the joyous sights
and sounds!
Say what more than dream of Eden, now my wondering
gaze astounds ;
Shafts of cocoa trees run lightly down the aisles of
tropic land,
Ranging stately with their columns dark the pillared
palm-trees stand.
Swift we left the ship, and landing trod these islands
all enchanted,
Gorgeous freightage of rich flowers down the laden-
branches slanted.
Fruits that sell for gold in England lay neglected on
the earth,
Golden grain o'er all the valleys laughed to scorn the
dread of dearth ;
Golden globes of pines broke laughing through their
leaves of emerald hue,
Banyans, mangoes, plantains, tamarinds in their lush
profusion grew.
Strung to music fled the hours, lapsing ran their golden
sands,
Swiftly ran the sparkling moments, softly sliding from
the hands

Life's reins lay idle on the necks of Life's reposing
    steeds,
While the charioteer lay dreaming 'midst the Aspho-
    delian meads;
All around me broke and murmured rushing currents of
    the life
The Arabian tales have painted with the Eastern magic
    rife.
All the Orient shed around me with its vari-coloured
    lights,
Seemed a dream remembered in a dream of the bright
    Arabian Nights;
When the perfumed air of even stole from all the
    gardens round,
Methought I was at Bagdad, in the caliph's haunted
    ground.

Now the moon of Java rising shines amid her purple
    skies,
Now the thicket's lamps are lighted tangled swarms of
    flashing flies;
Now the music shivers sweetly 'midst the murmur of the
    leaves,
Who remembers earth hath sorrows, who in grief or loss
    believes?
Every earthly care forgotten, every sorrow flies the
    world,

On the fragrant smoke that rising from each cigarette is
  curled;
There we linger sipping Mocha, drawn from berries of
  the South,
All Arabia in its perfume stealing sweetly o'er the
  mouth.
Happy comrades, silent smoke we, while sweet haunted
  dreams arise,
Of the perfumed lips of woman, of her darkly-gleaming
  eyes;
Happy comrades, could we ever glide thus softly down
  life's stream;
Happy comrades, could the future light all life with
  such a dream!

ANSWER TO LETTER FROM THE TROPICS.

I have read your glowing letter,
    I have pondered o'er its words,
Visioned all your tropic islands,
    With their topaz-painted birds.

Half I wished to see the vision
    With my grosser mortal sight,
Judge myself from seeing living
    'Midst your Edens of delight.

But for me the skies of England,
  And for me the English weather,
And the days that, ever changing,
  Scarce repeated come together.

O'er your groves of mangoes shining,
  Let your Eastern moon arise;
But for ever and for ever
  Shine o'er me from England's skies;

And for ever and for ever,
  Or while on earth I dwell,
'Gainst the cliffs of England let me
  Hear the English billows swell.

Break for me the grander ocean,
  Surge round me for evermore;
'Gainst the lintels of my dwelling
  Let loud London's ocean roar.

Set for me the sun of summer,
  Rise for me the summer moon;
Shine for me the lamps of London,
  Thro' the merry month of June;

Roar the knockers thro' the May-tide,
  Leap from door to door the thunder,
Let waxen lights shine overhead,
  And happy hearts beat under;

Wave the branches of the elm-trees,
  Droop the boughs with May-bloom laden,
Wed the lilac with the chestnut,
  And the cavalier with maiden.

When through Hyde Park alleys riding,
  Swarms the glittering cavalcade,
What to me your tropic islands,
  Or your dark-eyed Eastern maid?

And when change and quiet seeking
  From loud London's foam and hurry,
Give me Malvern's linking mountains,
  Or the autumn lanes of Surrey.

Are your tropic blossoms lovely
  As the bloom of Malvern vale,
"Summer snow of apple blossoms"
  Shedding fragrance on the gale?

Blows the tropic air as freshly,
  Bringing life to heart and cheek,
As the balmy breeze that meets me
  From each glorious Malvern peak?

Or from Surrey land enchanted,
  Of the poet and the muse,
From the groves of happy Twickenham
  Or of Ditton let me choose.

So the land that I was born in,
  And the land I love the best,
May for ever be my dwelling
  Be the soil where I shall rest !

Thus I answer to your praises,
  Praising England evermore,
Over every tropic island,
  Over every Eastern shore.

THE BLACKBIRD'S SONG.

I WANDERED abroad that morning,
  For my spirits were restless and sad,
With a sense of a something scorning
  The sober life I had had ;

And the springtide was bright around me,
  And the orchards were all a foam ;
But the beauty that once had bound me
  Seemed as dead as my life at home.

With scornful eyes I went gazing
  On the wealth of the landscape round ;
Nothing I saw won my praising,
  There was something I had not found.

For something my heart was yearning,
    For something my spirit was faint,
There was something I longed to be learning—
    I never was meant for a saint.

The blackbird could teach me that lesson
    'Midst the blanch of the white apple sprays,
In the flush and the thrill of that season,
    In the joy of those young April days,

He singeth aloud, but not lonely,
    He singeth of love to his mate,
He singeth of love, of love only,
    He singeth, and I hear my fate ;

For, swift she is coming, she's coming
    Where the meadow-path runs to the stile,
And the blackbird my story is summing,
    As he telleth his own the while.

Oh, love, I remember that morning ;
    Oh, love, shall you ever forget,
In the light and the flash of its dawning
    In the meadows, how you and I met ?

How you taught me the lesson I wanted,
    But first we passed into the wood,
Where the sunbeams' gold fingers were slanted
    To point where the summer-house stood.

Since that lesson's grown perfect by practice,
    You taught me of wooing and winning,
You taught me too well, that the fact is—
    On you be the sin of my sinning;

On you be the sin of my sinning,
    Whose looks lured and led me along;
Tho', as all things must have a beginning,
    Let us both blame that wicked bird's song.

IMPROMPTU,

On seeing the Trees of Onslow Square covered with Blossoms in March.

I saw pink blossoms flushing bloom,
    Pale March to May seek to beguile,
While, over Onslow Square, the gloom
    Of Winter caught the spring-tide's smile.

And strangers passing may have deemed
    It was the climate or the air;
But I knew why those blossoms bloomed,
    For Faucit's glance had fallen there.

TO MISS HELEN FAUCIT.

December 19th, 1866.

A PILGRIM once again I come
　To that enchanted shrine,
Which holds to-night all that my life
　Has held as most divine.

Ring, magic bell, and curtain rise,
　O give her to these eyes !
Though seen a thousand times, she still
　Would bring a sweet surprise.

My heart would hear her from my grave—
　Would hear her and rejoice—
Would hear her step, and beat again
　To music of her voice.

But O to live and hear her speak—
　To live and see her face—
To live and watch her move to-night,
　Orbed with divinest grace—

Is life, with cup so brimming full,
　A thousand common years
Could not contain its sum of bliss,
　Or value its sweet tears.

But list! what music steals on night,
    Enchanting all the earth ?
Nay, music was not born till now,
    And in those words has birth.

'Tis Juliet; but such Juliet scarce
    E'en Shakspeare's self hath wrought,
He shadowed but the vision's half,
    The other Faucit brought.

She rises on the night as rose,
    In the old pagan dream,
The flash of snow on golden sands,
    From ocean's spray the gleam.

Of Aphrodite's wreathing arms
    Upon the moonlit shore ;
The vision ages consecrate
    In pagan poet's lore.

So rises Juliet on the wave
    Of Shakspeare's golden verse ;
A woman flushed with Romeo's love,
    A child still to her nurse.

So, bathed in moonlight, steals she forth
    To wrap the soul in bliss,
And almost make us wish the stage
    Would yield no scene but this.

Till, 'mid the thick of leafy woods,
From tree to tree there runs
The Rosalind, who dwells for aye
'Neath Arden's summer suns.

What breezes ever blow afresh
From Arden's haunted green!
In Memory's glades how often I
Shall meet again that scene!

The cowslips fleck the grassy banks,
The hunter winds his horn,
The wild deer flies away afar,
The ground is left forlorn;

Till, steals there in, with archest grace,
That bright and genial boy,
To mock us with idyllic life
We never may enjoy;

For forests that we roam will ne'er
Be green as Arden's wood;
The oak and elm-tree stand not now
As they in Arden stood.

The huntsmen ne'er again will come
To dine as they dined there;
The green leaves shelter not such men,
The wood yields not such fare.

The witty words and wise that fell
    From Touchstone's Jacques' lips,
No more will wing them 'mid the glades,
    Where modern traveller dips.

And Rosalind, she never lived
    But in one golden dream,
Where forest life was glorified
    With forest tree and stream.

Not so; she lives again to-night,
    She moves before me now,
And Arden's turf is 'neath her feet.
    Its sun is on her brow.

And though the dream will fade anon,
    Yet life is not all bare,
While London holds one magic home,
    And while is worshipp'd there

Our English Helen, fairer far
    Than she the Greek ideal,
Though haloed whitely through the glare
    Of torches hymeneal,

That lighted to her bridal bed,
    Then wrapt the world in flames,
As Greek fought Trojan, claiming back
    His queen of Grecian dames.

Oh, fairest flower of all the earth!
Oh, violet of the world!
Let me rest here, near thy sweet grace,
    Still be my tent unfurled.

Nay, it is o'er, the curtain falls,
    The sun sets from my breast,
And life moves on, and I near thee
    Can never have my rest.

Once more within the street I stand,
    Thy light is now afar;
Life closes round me cold and drear,
    With its ignoble jar.

THE KINGDOM OF POWDERED HAIR.

There's a kingdom unsung in the poet's verse,
    You may search and not find it there;
But the poets were fools who no mention made
    Of the kingdom of powdered hair.

Once its realms were ruled by the queens of the earth,
    Look on Reynolds' canvas, and there
See the stately forms of the beautiful dames
    In that kingdom of powdered hair.

See the statesman and hero born to command,
  By the right of that royal air,
Of the princely men whom Sir Joshua limned
  In his kingdom of powdered hair.

There are Gainsborough's ladies in loveliest guise,
  And, looking around, tell me where
Are the women now found to compare with those
  In the kingdom of powdered hair?

Those beauties are faded—those heroes are dead,
  And the grace and the grandeur there
Have fled, like a dream, with the actors who lived
  In the kingdom of powdered hair.

But a memory lives of that haunted past
  In the precincts of charmed May Fair,
In whose underground regions you still may find
  Thrives a kingdom of powdered hair.

And beyond it, still stretching away to the north—
  Ay, e'en northward of Cavendish Square,
O'er the acres green of the Regent's Park,
  Spreads the kingdom of powdered hair.

From the farthermost west of Tyburnian homes,
  To the Bond Street side of May Fair,
You may track its dominion, nor reach the end
  Of the kingdom of powdered hair.

Majestic this realm is of scarlet and gold,
  And of lords and their ladies fair,
Who are waited upon by the glorified men
  Of this kingdom of powdered hair.

Of stature the tallest, of stateliest mien,
  Each Narcissus seems fully aware
That he is the man to be held *sans pareil*
  In the kingdom of powdered hair.

You may talk of the cows in fair Devon's fields ;
  But the calves beyond all compare
Are those of the Johnnies, *ces enfants gâtés*,
  Of the kingdom of powdered hair.

Whene'er in my rambles I chance to espy
  Their forms lounging in street or square,
I fancy Adonis reviving, yet lives
  In the kingdom of powdered hair.

And when they leap up on the carriage-board swift,
  A sight in the summer-tide rare,
I fancy them love-birds enchanted to men,
  In the kingdom of powdered hair.

O, woe for the day when reform shall encroach
  On the precincts of dear May Fair,
And shall sweep to the limbo of hoop and of patch
  My pet kingdom of powdered hair !

AUSTRIAN LAYS.

MARIA ANTOINETTE AT HER TRIAL.

" STAND forth, thou widow Capet, now, and hear thy
    doom declared !
Stand forth, thou Messalina ! thou shalt least of all be
    spared !
No wretch so steeped in guilt as thou, debaucher of thy
    child,
No harlot of the lowest lot with crime like thine
    defiled.
Stand forth ! " they shout ; she hears their yell, she
    stands within their lair,
A hundred faces press around, ablaze with hellish
    glare,
A hundred wolfish hearts athirst to slake their ravening
    hate
With blood of that lone woman, who comes forth to
    hear her fate.

She standeth forth with stately step, and with a regal
    mien,
As though that day of all her days had made her most
    a queen ;
The aureole of martyrdom seems to quiver round her
    brow,

And Austria's daughter, France's queen, she stands
before them now ;
The Hapsburg blood will dye no more the pallor of her
cheek,
But all its currents at her heart—she is no longer
weak.
Yet who can tell what visions now that haughty
woman sees
Of Trianon and Fontainebleau, and the gorgeous
Tuileries,
Of days when she was fairest of the fair that met her
glance,
The Dauphin's bride, the future queen of his resplen-
dent France ;
Of farther days, and more remote, when young, and
gay, and wild,
Within Vienna's pleasant walls she dwelt a happy
child ;
Of her wooing and her wedding, and her bridegroom's
careless mien,
That flowered into love at last, the truest earth has
seen ;
Of the crowds that thronged around her, of the love
she won from men,
Of the sudden change that followed, and the clouds
that gathered then,
Of Böhmer's diamond necklace, and De Rohan's cruel
cheat,

And the fatal mazes woven round by De La Motte's
    deceit;
Of the plots that blasted all her bliss, of the thunder-
    bolt that fell,
Of the deep, relentless surging of the mob in endless
    swell
That broke upon her palace walls, and swept her state
    away,
And left the stricken woman they have doomed to
    death to-day?

It may be so that all the past thus rushed upon her
    then,
That the joybells of her happy youth were ringing o'er
    again,
When the tocsin of her doom was heard amid exulting
    cries,
As the city's shout of gladness was flung upward to
    the skies.
Oh! fallen city, thus to shout at her majestic woe—
Oh! tiger hearts, no shame to feel, no pity now to
    show.
Oh! cowards, base and cruel, with no touch of man-
    hood's grace—
She who was late the brilliant queen of France's fickle
    race.
It matters not; with fearless heart she stands, and
    tranquil brow,

Grief's cup is drained to the last drop—they cannot
    hurt her now.
She stands sublimed by awful grief to that majestic
    state
Where suffering is a kingdom, and afflictions slaves that
    wait;
And their fiendish eyes are quailing, and they dare not
    meet the glance
Of pity from the pitying eyes of the martyred Queen of
    France.

AN INCIDENT OF 1859.

An Austrian and an Englishman
    Sat round the tavern board;
One claimed Victoria for his queen,
    One owned the Kaiser, lord.

One praised far London's mighty town,
    And one Vienna's grace;
One toasted his fair Austrian maid,
    One loved an English face;

But still their hearts grew warm together,
    And as each gazed on other,
Face looked to face with earnest eyes,
    As brother unto brother.

And still they quaffed the blood-bright wine,
    Their hearts flushed warm and mellow;
And each of other silent said,
    " He is a right good fellow."

The Frenchman—thought the English youth—
    Has soft and subtle grace,
Italia's son a dreamy light
    Of beauty on his face.

My English brethren I can trust,
    And yet I know not how;
There is a something franker far
    Upon the Austrian brow.

The Austrian soldier thought him back—
    I shall not find another
So honest, true, and trusty as
    Is this my English brother.

My Austrian comrades have for me
    Frank heart and ready hand,
There are no truer men on earth
    Than in the Austrian land.

Bavaria has a noble race
    Of hearty men and true,
But something kindles more my heart
    In England's eye of blue.

He must not leave us, he is young,
   And rich, and free, and brave ;
"Come, brother, come, and join our ranks
Against the Italian slave."

Fierce flashed the English eye, and broke
   Like lightning on the air ;
" The Kaiser's slave of Freedom's sons
   May well speak thus, I swear.

" But he forgets how English blood
   In Freedom's cause is shed,
And how to sacred Freedom still
   Old England's heart is wed."

The Austrian sprang upon his feet,
   And brow and cheek grew white ;
" The answer to your insult must
   Be writ in blood to-night."

They fought, the lads who late had been
   In friendship knit so warm,
Until one reckless word awoke
   Each noble nature's storm.

They fought, and one fell ne'er again
   From the wet sward to rise,
Or meet his comrade's grasp, or see
   His distant English skies.

But from that day the Austrian lad
  Grew dull and cold as ice ;
Nor wine could flush him, nor his brain
  Be fevered by the dice.

Some care pressed heavy on his heart,
  And weighed him to his grave ;
But his last words were—" I am free,
  No longer despot's slave !"

Did Austria's noble Kaiser catch
  Some echo from that heart,
That won his young and princely soul
  To choose its godlike part?

To be the leader of the kings
  Who rule in Freedom's name ;
And despot only o'er those hearts
  Fed with love's willing flame.

I know not when for Freedom's cause,
  His royal heart first burnt ;
But this I know, that none so well
  Has her high lesson learnt.

The noblest prince on earth I hold,
  And worthily adored,
Is he proud Austria proudly calls
  Her Kaiser, King, and Lord.

" POOR MAX. !"

Poor Max. !—all his vision departed—
 High vision of good to be done—
And half, as he writes, broken-hearted,
 Little thinks that the new-risen sun

Might flash on that morn with fresh lustre—
 Might feed a more passionate flame—
Might strike through the stars' fervent cluster
 With a heat to their outermost frame.

For recalling the morn that his rays
 Passed in mercy from Calvary's mount,
He may reckon in vain o'er the days
 Of the seventeen centuries' count.

No martyrs have risen to fill them
 With glory as One filled the first ;
Though the Church has been thirsty to kill them,
 And priestcraft has dealt them its worst.

But now, from this morn through all morrows
 Earth owns a new martyr arisen,
As an Emperor, crowned with his sorrows,
 Comes Max. from his Mexican prison.

" Poor Max. !" ay, thy heart's fervent letter
 Men ages to come will remember,
And appraising thee, deem but one better,
 The Sun of the Christian December.

"Poor Max.!" not Carlotta shall fold thee
  So close to her desolate heart,
As the heart of all manhood shall hold thee
  In the niche where its heroes have part.

GARIBALDIAN LAYS.

MENTANA.

YES, they are broken and shattered,
  Scattered to right and to left,
Conquered, and helpless, and flying,
  Of hope and of glory bereft.

They were wild—they were rash—nay, insane,
  For a conflict most hopeless arrayed
With the might of an empire against them,
  And by their own monarch betrayed.

Yet they fought for a cause that was glorious ;
  Should this be quite left out of mind
When we scoff at these poor Garibaldians,
  As madmen, misguided, and blind ?

'Tis true, we are wiser than they,
  We Englishmen living at home ;
We may be—Victoria our Queen—
  We may be—with London for Rome.

But shall we, the happy and loyal,
  In appraising them, wholly condemn?
Have we no reminiscence that leaves us
  Some feeling of pity for them?

Did we never struggle for freedom—
  Did we never suffer and bleed;
How ranks England, the queen of the nations,
  In right of her Protestant creed?

Not the creed of the bigot I speak of—
  Not the creed of this Church or the other:
But the creed that will leave to no priesthood
  Or pontiff permission to smother.

The will of a nation demanding,
  In accents not doubtful in sound,
That its destinies have their fulfilment,
  Its legitimate longings be crowned.

In such accents has Italy pleaded,
  With such force in her passionate voice,
Demanding for Rome as Venetia,
  The right to her freedom of choice—

The right to take rank with her sisters,
  No longer sit lonely apart,
The Niobe still among cities,
  Chained, captive, and stricken at heart.

What had Venice of slavery like hers,
   'Neath the Kaiser's beneficent rule?
As well match the wretch in the dungeon
   With the disciplined lad in the school.

What had Florence or Parma to chafe at—
   Nay, rather, what did they not lose?
Yet they banished their archduke and duchess,
   That they might with one Italy choose.

And what is the Pope more than Kaiser?
   Why, when archdukes resign, should he reign—
Why sit ever, like some Fate opposing
   " Non possumus," dungeon, and chain?

Nay; and fierce burnt the flame at their hearts,
   Why waste we fair time in the asking?
Let the war-flame be lighted, that soon
   Will see Italy in its rays basking.

O, onwards for Italy, brothers,
   Garibaldi himself leads the van—
Garibaldi! the word was as magic,
   The battle seemed won to each man.

And onwards they rushed, with hearts flaming,
   To find hearts in slavery dead,
To strike for the caitiffs, who folded
   Their arms while these struggled and bled.

To find that their sovereign had lured them
　To betray in that hour of danger,
And that, masked by the forces of Rome,
　Stood the terrible strength of the stranger.

Well, it is over, and requiems sung
　In the chapels of London and Rome,
O'er the men who fell fighting in slavery's cause,
　Against all we most cherish at home.

And shall we sing over these wild Garibaldians
　No requiem straight from the heart?
Though others disown them, yet shall we not own
　　them,
　As brothers in whom we've some part?

Let us blame them for folly and rashness in hoping
　To carry a desperate cause;
When succeeding, we know how our country had
　　led off
　The chorus of freemen's applause.

Yet, at least, be we thankful, as deeper and darker
　Falls the curse of the pontiff o'er Rome,
That such heroes once freed us, and freed us for
　　ever
　From pontiff and priestetaft at home.

IS IT OVER?

Is it over?—nay, nay, 'tis not over,
 Though the priest sit triumphant awhile;
Though tyranny's mildew may moulder
 Roman earth for a seventy mile.

Yet, brothers, be sure 'tis not over;
 And the land where our heroes have stood
Shall blossom and ripen to harvest,
 Made richer by patriots' blood.

Where they stood with the Zouaves before them,
 And the might of fair France masked behind,
Be sure we shall come to raise o'er them
 Glad shouts of Italians combined.

Be sure that Mentana shall echo
 From fortress to fortress our guns,
And Monte Rotondo's loud volleys
 Shall welcome her conquering sons.

But oh, our brothers, the Romans,
 Shall your heads not then droop and sink down,
Who heard of our fighting, and stood
 With arms folded and calm in your town?

Who stood your oppressors to welcome,
 And, dressing with flowers your chains,
Received your Zouaves fresh from slaughter
 Of brothers with flattering strains?

Alas! what for Freedom can fit ye,
  What re-gild your degenerate name ;
What efface the black memory clinging,
  Of that day dark with dye of your shame ?

Ye knew we were coming to save you,
  Ye knew we bore Liberty's letters,
Credentials of Italy eager to free you
  From weight of long centuries' fetters.

Nay, scorn burns too fierce to reproach ye ;
  But oh, our brothers, the brave,
Did ye shed your young blood, are ye lying
    beneath us,
  For sake of the caitiff and slave?

How despised of the Tuscan henceforth ye shall be,
  Still slaves to your slavery cleaving,
While Italy sighs as she clusters the leaves
  In her garland of Liberty's weaving—

The laurel leaves, bearing, in letters of gold,
  The names of each fair sister city ;
So while Italy sings 'neath her garland of green,
  Let Rome have our dirge for a ditty.

But we shall avenge you, our brothers, the brave,
  We shall trophy the field of your slaughter ;
We shall write your dear names on St. Angelo's fort,
  When victory Rome's pardon has bought her.

THE PONTIFF'S PRAYER.

The pontiff's hands on the altar are laid, and his eyes
   are raised to heaven ;
" Exsurge Domine," listening then, if an answer from
   France were given.

For from heaven I think, were an answer sent, it
   would be in the crash of the thunder,
And the lightning's flash on the mitred head of the
   hypocrite kneeling under.

The meek high priest with the saintly smile, so hard to
   distinguish from smirk—
The meek high priest, who the Zouaves has sent to do
   his merciless work.

And they are smiting, and striking, and shooting, and
   stabbing, and slaying,
And he, at the altar kneeling, to God as to devils is
   praying.

As a Jew might have prayed to his God in the mist of
   the ages past,
Prays the vicar of Christ in a Christian fane, and to
   this it has come at last.

That the vicar of Christ prays ignoring Christ's teach-
   ing, and name, and behest,
Prays for cursing and smiting from heaven as a heathen
   or Jew at the best.

Could he glance in a vision down vistas that slope to a
 far-lying past ;
Could he see in a garden's deep thickets the form of a
 Sufferer cast ;

Could the voice of that Sufferer resounding roll down
 the long corridor's length,
From century leading to century, in deep echoes still
 gathering strength ;

Could he pray then with hands on the altar, could he
 pray with those sounds in his ears,
With their closes of silence unbroken, save by fall of
 the Sufferer's tears ?

Could he pass in a trance from the present, o'erscaling
 the barriers of time ;
Could the centuries wheeling them backwards bid the
 hours of old again chime ;—

He would see his meek Master still praying, tho' angels,
 if summoned, would aid him ;
" Thy will, oh, my Father, be done !" in the sight of
 the men who betrayed him.

But no; every word of the Saviour, His gesture, and
 accents, and speech,
Are lost in the volleying chassepots, are drowned in the
 tramp and the screech.

Where thick in the smoke and confusion, commingled
    in fight and in slaughter,
The sons of our Italy fall, for the cause of our Italy's
    daughter,

Shot thro' by the troops of the pontiff, blasphemer of
    Christ at Christ's altar ;
Still the brave Garibaldian columns stand firmly toge-
    ther, nor falter.

Badly trained, badly armed, young in years, mere boys,
    some who fell fighting there,
Still the day will be theirs, for the Zouaves are breaking
    their ranks in despair.

But surging, and swaying, and breaking 'neath the red
    Garibaldians' advance,
Lo! denser and darker behind them, thick array of the
    soldiers of France,

And thundering volleys of chassepots, with the pope's
    prayers, are mounting on high :
And shot down, and slaughtered, and trampled, the
    brave Garibaldians lie.

And the caitiffs of Rome are applauding as their con-
    querors sweep thro' her streets,
But cursing and hate in their hearts, as their last hope
    of liberty fleets ;

For they know they are false to their brothers, their
    brothers who died in their youth,
And bright hopes and high visions, died fighting for
    freedom, and country, and truth.

And the pope he is singing Te Deums, and the priests
    their thanksgivings are chanting,
As fast sinks the sun and the shadows of night o'er the
    town still the pontiff's are slanting;

And with it sinks still swifter downwards the sun of a
    fond hope arisen,
That Romans, like other Italians, might rise and come
    out of their prison.*

* In this and the preceding lay I have endeavoured to give
expression to the sentiments a Garibaldian may be well supposed to
have entertained at the close of the disastrous campaign of last
autumn, but I wish to guard against the possible conclusion that
these sentiments are in every respect identical with my own. The
first lay of the three sufficiently conveys my own feeling on the
subject.

ENGLISH LAYS.

HARROW-ON-THE-HILL.

THE day was fading swiftly along the bright
　　Durance,
The brilliant day of Montpelier, the day of southern
　　France;
And the friend I loved lay dying, and, save that I stood
　　near,
There was none to bend above him—there was none to
　　shed a tear.
And his thoughts were rushing homewards, and he
　　feebly, faintly said,
"Oh! friend who loved me living, forsake me not when
　　dead;
Oh, lay me not to rest in a strange and foreign
　　grave,
But bear me where the English elm may o'er my tomb-
　　stone wave—
The English elm I see it on a spot remembered still,
In the old churchyard of Harrow—of Harrow-on-the-
　　Hill.

"Last night I dreamt I saw it, the well-remembered
　　place,
Each field that lay in distance, each hedgerow I could
　　trace;

Once more a boy, I wandered through the sheltered
 lanes around,
Where the yellow leaves of autumn were falling to the
 ground ;
And the fragrance and the stillness, and the sadness on
 the air,
Made a weight upon my spirit that was more than I
 could bear ;
And I felt a sudden longing to leave this wondrous
 earth,
Too weary far to listen to its voices and its mirth.
I longed to lay my limbs at rest, and be for ever
 still
In the old churchyard of Harrow—of Harrow-on-the-
 Hill.

" And, Arthur, you have loved me since the day that
 first we met,
Too long a love, too dear an one for either to
 forget ;
I know you'll often think of me, and life will be more
 drear
When you go forth without the friend of many a happy
 year.
So look me truly in the eyes, and hold, hold firm my
 hand,
And promise you will bear me to my own loved English
 land—

The land where you and I as lads have often walked
    together
In the summer, and the autumn, and the hearty winter
    weather;
And clasp my hand more firmly, and vow more truly
    still,
That I shall rest at Harrow—at Harrow-on-the-Hill.

" There,'a lady living lonely, will weep for many a day
When they tell her, when they tell her, Arthur, I am
    passed away;
She wept wild tears of grief one morning long ago,
And I turned away the swifter that I might not see her
    woe.
Oh! my mother, had I stayed with thee within that
    peaceful home,
But who can check the young heart when it bids the
    young man roam?
And I think she will forgive me when you go to her and
    say,
' Though his youth was very wayward, and he
    wandered far away,
Yet in dying, to his friend, it was his last and only
    will,
To rest near you at Harrow—at Harrow-on-the-Hill.' "

THE GREAT SEAL OF ENGLAND.

Part I.—The Keepers of the Seal.

O give me now a subject fit for rapturous strain of
    verse,

Some glorious deed of warrior or of statesman to
    rehearse ;

Thanks, Lilian, thanks ; and Alice, too, 'tis a glorious
    list you give

Of the great old Dead of England, of their words that
    burn and live ;

And the very page seems purple, as I read the names
    you write,

And the flame of England's glories seems to touch it
    with its light ;

And the pearls of stately memories, and the diamonds
    of her fame,

Cluster circling thick and glorious round each old
    historic name ;

But a sudden subject strikes me, and I throw your
    themes aside,

And my bosom glows with rapture, and my heart beats
    high with pride,

As eight dead centuries start to life, and each its tale
    reveals

Of England's great Lord Keepers—the Lord Keepers of
    her Seals.

How gloriously their ranks live out, as through the mist
    of ages
Leaps the light of England's story on the long line of
    her Sages,
Who shaped their era's fashion, stamping clean and
    without flaw,
On the passions seething round them the strong seal of
    English law.
As from chain of Alpine mountains peak after peak
    receding,
Cut clear against the sky will rise the last peak as the
    leading,
Yet one will catch a richer light upon its snow-wreathed
    head,
And one will tell more whitely out against the evening
    red;
So 'midst this courtly conclave with proud faces strongly
    cast
On the rich horizon glowing with the memories of the
    past,
Some, 'gainst the splendour of their time, will rise with
    nobler name,
With a whiter wreath of moral worth, or a fuller flush
    of fame.
As where through Time's long vistas sinks the sunlight
    sadly down,
O'er the battle-field of Hastings, where the Norman won
    his crown;

O'er the plain strewn with the dying 'gainst the red
    orb sinking low,
Whiter gallops through the distance the white steed his
    Normans know,
As the gallant Keeper Odo, with his bâton borne in
    hand,
Leads the van of Norman conquest leaping o'er the
    Saxon land;
Or where—Time's chariot chiming down the gliding
    groove of years—
Comes again the trumpets' revel—rush of battle—clang
    of spears,
Where we still from Shakespeare's clarion catch the
    cheer of Harry's call,
Our valiant Monmouth Harry, over Harry Hotspur's fall;
There wise in council as in war rides 'midst the ringing
    peals,
The brave Lord Keeper Gascoigne—the Lord Keeper of
    the Seals.

And names more glorious yet stand out upon our
    history's page,
Through the darkness brighter flashing on the forehead
    of the age;
And the silent air is stirring with sweet murmurs as of
    song,
And the fervent words of poets, wed to music, float
    along;

There are Hatton's name, and Verulam's, and he who
    went before,
Still clinging to his youth's false creed, misguided
    saintly More;
And as the changing shadows drift across their age's dial,
We hear one chant in Chelsea church, and touch his
    silver viol,
We hear the other's golden speech roll music on the air,
And read the sole page in the world that with Shake-
    speare's can compare.
And round that rich roll-call of Fame what sadder
    memories wait
Of the high in human nature, of the dark in human
    fate,
What thought of those who laboured long, who toiled
    out life in vain,
To trembling hand and shattered nerve, and dark dis-
    tempered brain !
O, well sang one her lovely lay, whose glance surveying
    met
The dark and solemn buildings round the Temple's
    fountain set—

    " What struggles, what hope, what despair may have been
    Where sweep those dark branches of shadowy green !"

And there are those who bounded on, who touched the
    golden goal,
While radiant yet around their brows shone Youth's
    bright aureole,

Who mounted to the Marble Chair, who snatched the
  Crimson Purse,
And lived to find that brilliant prize to them life's
  heaviest curse.
Such the glittering thread of gladness—such the dark
  thread Fortune steals,
In the web she weaves the Keepers—the Lord Keepers
  of the Seals.

And pondering thus their story o'er, we find the past
  has led
To the deep abyss that severs still the living from the
  dead,
While standing on a neck of earth, enough for his light
  weight,
One old man's hands are stretching to the hands he
  grasped so late—
One link still left in that old man to join us to the past,
To the giant forms of story amidst whom his youth was
  cast ;
And, bent with him o'er Time's abyss, we fancy we
  can hear
The surge and sweep of many a speech, long faded from
  the ear—
Hear the silver tone of Brougham—see the flush to
  cheek has flown,
And the listener's eye is kindling as he claims it for
  his own,

As the years yield up their echoes of his old familiar art,
Of that facile voice's charming, winding round his
    hearer's heart;
Catch the sound of Eldon's weeping through the silence
    of the Court,
Hear the clarion ring of Erskine, as he answers back in
    sport;
Listen, hushed for Lyndhurst's accents, that none
    hearing could forget—
Accents lingering, in their beauty, round the Senate
    chambers yet:
Start to see the angry eye-balls flash their lightnings
    from the chair,
As the thunder-bursts of Thurlow sweep the tempest-
    laden air;
Thus bending o'er Time's dark abyss, to Fancy's ear
    arise
The mingled voices of the men long vanished from our
    eyes;
And thus and thus the centuries run, and each its tale
    reveals
Of England's great Lord Keepers—the Lord Keepers of
    her Seals.

Part II.—*The Seal.*

Nor less than of the Keepers of the Seal itself my
    lay—

The great Broad Seal of England—Victoria's Seal to-
    day ;

But e'er from graver's subtle hand had the ductile gem
    received,

In the lines of truth and beauty, the fair face no loss
    then grieved—

The Queen's face, that smiled in gladness as she met her
    subjects' face—

The girl's face, that hid its roses blushing 'neath the
    bridal lace—

The wife's face, that looked in rapture, as the crown of
    all her pride

Was the husband guarding ever, loving ever, at her
    side,

Ere hers, how many features had across that signet
    played,

As the course of centuries graved it with the monarchs
    they had made ;

Since the saintly Edward's image rose to vision on its
    sealing,

All the kingly race of England—all her royal line
    revealing ;

It has seen the star rise redly, it has seen it darkly
    set,

With the fortunes waxing, waning of each proud Plan-
    tagenet;

Of the great and gallant Edward, dear to Froissart's
    splendid pen—

Of the gentle, lamb-like Edward, done to death by
    savage men—

Of the proud and princely Edward, shining forth from
    every page—

Of the grand chivalric story of that grand, chivalric
    age—

It has caught the red rose colour, it has borne the
    stainless white

Of the rival roses mingled after Bosworth's brilliant
    fight—

It has imaged noble Richmond, the first Tudor England
    knew,

And the handsome bluff eighth Harry, with his eye of
    merry blue;

It has borne the stamp of Mary, and her butcher lord
    of Spain,

Our flawless Seal of England, save for their ignoble
    stain—

And hers, the monarch of all monarchs that have ever
    reigned on earth,

Great lioness of England, never man excelled in
    worth;

She who drew her father's sword, she who sware her
    father's oath,

Royal Henry's virgin daughter, royal England's spot-
less troth—

She whom half of royal Europe, vainly wooing, wished
to wed;

But her heart was wed to England, "I am England's
bride," she said;

And Old England's heart still holds her proudest name
of all her story,

Silver star of Tudor, blazoned on her purple field of
glory,

Like the lily, lone and stately, towered high that virgin
head,

Regnant rose that royal spirit, yet her woman's heart
had bled

When the love of Leicester touched her in the blossom
of her youth,

And the love of Essex wooed her with false mien of
manly truth;

Till the recreant and the braggart stung her royal heart
to madness,

And o'er her dark delirium fell Death's purple pall in
sadness;

And when her seal of fifty years broke 'neath the
craftsman's blow,

How many a gallant English heart sank stricken then
and low;

How many an eye grew dim with tears, when it could
no longer trace

The old familiar features of Queen Bess's cherished
  face.

Then flitting o'er its surface passed each prince of
  Stuart line,

With the proud majestic presence of the lords of right
  divine,

The sixth Scotch James, and proud false Charles, and
  Charles's graceless sons,

Dark shadows swiftly drifting as the tale of history
  runs ;

Till borne on tide of Fortune rose the wished-for wave
  at last,

Hurrah ! hurrah ! the Nassau flag meets Devon's
  friendly blast ;

And the Seal that James, in flying, had for ever
  thought to hide,

Rose for England's great law-saver—rose for William
  and his bride ;

And the strong cut face of Nassau, and the beauteous
  Stuart Mary,

Lent a legend more romantic than all tale of knight and
  fairy,

Graved a story dear to-day to every English heart and
  home,

Dearer thinking of those slaughtered by the Zouave
  force of Rome ;

And their faces fading from it rose the comely face of
  Anne—

Of the good queen, fairly fashioned on the good old
English plan,
Somewhat stubborn, somewhat wanting in that finer
tact and grace,
Loved through length and breadth of England on a
dearer, fairer face ;
But a woman still true-hearted, of the English blood and
name,
Heiress of the God-anointed Stuarts, and of Hyde's
historic fame.

And thus and thus the story runs, face after face is
graved
Of the kings whom England honoured, of the prince
who England saved ;
And the four queens regnant long discrowned, and the
one who rules to-day,
Round whom her nobles cluster, and for whom her
people pray,
Hoping still to see her breaking from the vigil of her
sadness,
And with her subjects sharing as in sorrow so in
gladness.

HYDE PARK IN MAY.

Now blooms the lilac, and on leafy thrones,
'Midst green savannahs rise the chestnut cones;
The milky hawthorn strews her summer snow,
And gold sierras of laburnum glow;
Now Bond Street bobbies boldly dash athwart
The ranks of carriages they keep apart;
Heroic plunge they 'midst the lock of wheels,
'Midst that same lock the thief unnoted steals.
Now fill the benches Marshall's doors provide
With the matched footmen, each a household's pride;
Now like a pear-tree after April's showers,
Burst Brandon's windows into sudden flowers;
And Foster, Eagle each with rival bloom,
Paints the rich spray, and tints the snowy plume;
Now drapes Elise her casements with that lace,
Whose price is fabulous as Lady ——'s face.
Nor Howell rusts the lustre of thy name,
Resplendent now with half a century's fame,
While Hancock, Boore, and Mortimer display
A Rajah's fortune on each glittering tray.
Now blaze the ball-rooms with their contrast keen
To conjure memories of a different scene,
As some young bride with dazzled eyes recalls
Her evenings pent within the vicarage walls;
Or Doctor's daughter from her village borne,
Looks back on visions she has learnt to scorn,

Of rooms some twelve feet wide by twenty long,
Crammed with their third-rate dull provincial throng.
Their few dim lights that show you but the gloom,
But hint at objects that they can't illume ;
A spinster aunt to play quadrilles all night,
Whose heart is heavy, and whose hand not light.
Such is the vision the young wife recalls
At memory's shaping of her girlhood's balls;
How different this from London's glad midnight,
When roars the knocker, shines the resplendent light,
When gorgeous liveries blaze around the hall,
And beauty, music, perfume every sense enthral,
As Fashion calls her titled crowds to meet
In Carlton Gardens or in Curzon Street.
Here borne on crescent wave of Folly's tide,
The village maiden shines the titled bride,
And but looks back to bless her stars, she sold
Her virgin beauty for her bridegroom's gold.
Thus pass in London gilded hours of night,
Nor morning ones less radiant take their flight;
Where fresh as roses May-fair maidens ride
Through Nature's carnival—the fair May-tide,
Down that famed Row where soon as comes the May,
Comes England's beauty in its proud array,
With ring and chime of that bright cavalcade
Of steed and groom, and cavalier and maid.
There he who loves his race to criticize,
Or views the world with jealous jaundiced eyes,

May find rich grist to feed his cynic mill,
And mangle reputations at his will.
To my mild mood, the figures come and go
Like some vast gay but harmless puppet-show;
There A——y passes with that air serene
Of calm assurance on his thoughtful mien,
Too grave, too earnest for his years, in sooth,
That should flush o'er with all the glow of youth;
Who learn to love him first learn to esteem,
And forced by him to be the thing you'd seem.
His lofty nature sways you to despise
All fawning arts, all artful courtesies;
Yet still you miss a something of that art
Which ere you know it steals away your heart;
And while confessing A—— is wise and good,
You feel you scarcely love him as you should;
While his most fervent followers own that still
Their hearts are less led captive than their will.
How different he from D——, who passes now
Smooth-tongued, cold-hearted, with a white bland
    brow;
You know, *sans doute*, the very man I mean,
Accomplished actor in life's every scene,
Who'll crush your heart out with his sweetest
    smile,
Whispering some well-turned compliment the while;
Yet flattered, honoured goes his prosperous life,
Bland husband to an acquiescent wife,

Indulgent father to a faultless child,
To studious servants softly phrased and mild,
Blessed with obedient servants, children, wife,
He well may play his good safe part in life ;
But thwarted, crossed by friend, or wife betrayed,
D—— is the stuff from which a Borgia's made ;
And once, indeed, to him there nearly came
The hour to turn his frosty soul to flame ;
Dishonour threatened, foe on foe assailed ;
But matched 'gainst all his matchless will prevailed,
The slander silenced, put his foes to flight,
And wrapped his secret in profoundest night.
See next, with buoyant step and laughing mien,
Gay, easy Myrtle shoot across the scene ;
But no ; 'tis but my memory sees him smile,
Or lounging, look across the Lady's Mile ;
Whose favouring glance a brighter blush awoke,
While hearts beat quicker if but Myrtle spoke.
How in those days I envied him his life,
A bachelor, who might select his wife
From out the fairest of the fair May Fair,
And need but choose to find acceptance there ;
But he, perchance, knew female arts too well
To yield his heart to any May Fair spell,
And so grew old, unloving and unwed,
Till his glad spirits, grace, and wit had fled.
What now are all advantages of youth,
But withered roses o'er a grave, in sooth ?

Who Myrtle sees to-day lean on the rail,
Sees how time takes the wind from manhood's sail.
What this bright Myrtle, this the Row's Le Beau,
With dress so careless, and with step so slow—
This Myrtle, who, with arm leaned on a friend,
Slow traverses the Mile from end to end,
And seems to see, with sad and restless stare,
Ghosts of dead fancies, vanished faces fair?
Strong contrast he to him who makes his boast,
The rudest muscle of that gallant host;
And breaks, each winter, some three hours ere nine,
Not ice of ceremony, but of Serpentine;
There lounges C——, whose mind's with memories
    writ
Of Gore-house suppers, and of D'Orsay's wit—
Days that the lovely Margaret held divine,
When Wellington brought incense to her shrine,
When Landor, Lyndhurst, Lytton spread her fame,
And the world crowding to her footstool came,
Passed swift—how swift the brilliance of her reign;
And now, by hastening currents of the Seine,
Beneath St. Germain, shadowed by its gloom,
Chambourcy whitely rears the lonely tomb,
Within whose chamber, folded side by side,
Sleep woman's loveliness and manhood's pride.
How one year's lapse on Lady —— has told;
Last year her ringlets black as midnight rolled,
And now run rippling in a flood of gold.

How young, how radiant, and how happy she,
Whose last stake played has won the wished-for *prix*.
Alas! when such the lesson she can teach,
Vain are all sermons that the preachers preach.
There, through all seasons, drives that portly dame,
For years companioned by the withered frame,
Which, though it semblance of her husband bore,
Some swore a mummy stuffed ten years or more ;
Now gone the mummy, smiling in its stead,
The young Adonis she has lately wed.
There, blending with the throng as it drifts by,
Prince Arthur, jovial Cambridge meet the eye—
There swift the steed bears by the boundary rails
Bright Lady Mary, with her heart in Wales.
In yon proud beauty's half-averted face,
The artless girl's of former days I trace ;
One season flashed she on the town's charmed eyes,
But London ball-rooms captured not the prize ;
'Twas Solent saw the wooing, saw the earl
Ten pearls exchanging for one priceless pearl ;
Knowing that of his lineage none had set
On fairer brow the W——n coronet.
What marvel is the scent lost to the pack,
And orthodoxy's hounds thrown off the track,
That they sweep not upon us when so near,
And yet in quiet walks Colenso here ?
I strain my ear if o'er the general hum
I catch their cry, and watch to see them come—

Watch to see C—p—n follow as they run ;
Bishop hunt bishop must be glorious fun.
But, O, how swiftly o'er the mind will pass,
Swift as the shadows o'er yon sunny grass,
The thoughts of those fair forms that come not now
To add their charm to that unrivalled show ;
Why name them ?   Some—one chief of all
Will start to memory ere her name can fall ;
E'en those who but her pictured face have seen,
Will conjure up the grace of Clementine.
Some, too, still live, but running off the line,
No more in alleys of Hyde Park shall shine—
Or shine, henceforth, but 'midst those lurid stars—
Those fierce, red planets, whose hot lustre mars
The milder radiance of our stainless dames,
As the rouged cheek each paler cheek outflames.
Thus lingering, musing o'er that glittering sight,
Thoughts, sad and mirthful, took alternate flight :
But shall I own that in my mind and heart,
Not mirth, but sorrow, held the larger part,
And, owned I pulpit, I could make stern speech
From the sad sermon Row and drive can preach ;
So much that's worthless, both in maid and man,
In raddled roué, hackneyed harridan—
In false, fair faces with their heartless smile,
Is seen from end to end of that short mile.
But there behold a sight to stir the heart,
The two great chieftains not ten yards apart,

G—— and D——, each with courteous brow,
From which is smoothed all opposition now ;
The great Whig party's great Whig leader seems
As one who to the future looks and dreams,
That, when the heat and fury of the fray
Die off, there yet will rise an ampler day ;
His cheek is pale and worn, his mouth is stern,
A leader who has seen the tide of victory turn—
Has seen low cunning, petty arts prevail,
And meets his rival fanned by victory's gale,
Yet in defeat's dark hour seems nobler far
Than he on whom shines Fortune's fairest star ;
From whose sly smile and lurking lids there start—
You almost hear the hiss, and see the dart—
The scorpion venom and the poisoned sting
Of the swift satire none like him can fling ;
Now on his lips, as hovering seems the lance
He fain would hurl, he meets his rival's glance ;
That o'er the present seeks the future years,
Where the rich guerdon of his hopes appears—
Where the long struggle in the glorious cause
Of Freedom conquers 'midst a world's applause ;
Say then, whose follower, if your choice were free,
The Victor's or the Vanquished's would you be ;
But now the sun sinks down, the crowd breaks up,
May Fair must dine, and Islington must sup.
The dapper clerks, who strut their little hour,
    Seek their cleaned gloves, and choose their ball-room
        flower ;   L

The *debutante* take counsel with her maid,
To be in this or that rich lace arrayed;
And all departing, divers ways must go,
While night and silence hold the empty Row.

THE LAST WORDS OF MARSHAL SAXE.

WHAT has my life been but a dream?
  Though beautiful, 'twas short;
Dreamed out between the sword's red gleam
  And revel of the Court.

So let it be—I would not change
  That life of sun and storm,
That burning blood, whose fever's range
  Kept all my passions warm,

For any even-tempered frame,
  Or calmly-pulsing blood;
Mine was a Man's life, all that came
  Of pleasure was its food.

Of wine and women, war and sport,
  I had and drank my fill;
I drained my cup of joys right off,
  And ne'er a drop did spill.

My fierce fast span of fifty years
  Was worth a dozen lives;
I shall not now shed any tears
  For any sin it hives.

What! weep that I have tasted all
    The world could give of bliss?
Fed lust, and found it never pall,
    And now lament for this?

What should a man do but live thus?
    Why waste a single day
Of all the days the gods give us
    To fight, and sweat, and slay?

And then to fling the red sword down,
    And 'midst the cannon's pause,
Snatch all the joys our life can crown,
    And laugh at monkish laws.

I tell you such a life is worth
    Ten hundred such as those
With which faint wretches turn the earth
    Into a monkish close.

White Virtue's lily never had
    For me a single charm;
Give me Lust's roses all unclad,
    And red as wine and warm.

So spake stout Konigsmark, and died--
    Blame him all ye who can;
But own those words of power and pride
    Came from an honest man.

And though since first suns set and rose,
    And moons did wane and wax,

Few wilder words have dropt than those
  Which fell from Marshal Saxe.

Yet own him one who in our days
  Would have done nobler work ;
A man who for no mortal's praise
  Would any duty shirk.

Own, too, each age and clime will chalk
  Their difference on the man ;
Making one century's Konigsmark
  Another's Wellington.

THE FAUN IN THE CAPITOL.

What glad and jocund thing is this
  That greets my vision now ?
What grace is in those pliant limbs,
  What sweetness on that brow !

What rose could ope with sweeter breath,
  O'er blown by the warm south ;
Than the sweet rose's fragrant bud,
  Of thy half-smiling mouth ?

I long to fold thee in my arms,
  And bid thy face to rest
For evermore, with that arch smile,
  Upon my yearning breast.

What art thou standing thus amidst
   The shapes of god and man
Quaint reminiscence in thy form
   Of the wood's rustic Pan ?

All the sweet dreams of pagan lore
   Seem lurking in thy mien ;
Sly hints, half-guesses, subtle charms
   Of essence epicene

Breathe from thy gracious form and face,
   Where the soft marble's yellow ;
Glows 'midst the glorious forms around,
   In beauty without fellow.

All odours from the fresh spring woods
   Of thyme, and moss, and flower,
Seem blown around thee by the grace
   Of Nature's woodland dower.

Play but a note on thy sweet pipe,
   And from their mossy cover
The hare will start—the rabbit leap—
   The greyhound jump them over.

The squirrel stand with beechen mast
   Untasted midst her paws ;
And all wild things come from their cells.
   Drawn by instinctive laws.

The spring sap in the thrilling pines,
   Will stir through all their branches

The wild deer pause in sight of bolt
    The following huntsman launches.

The stately stags will leaping press
    In wild crowds through the thicket,
O'er paling, fence, and rustic rail,
    Through every gate and wicket.

When all things love thee, why not I?
    Shall a cold creed forbid
That love should draw from thy fair form
    The mystic sweetness hid?

No; hear me now, dear Faun, forswear—
    And prick thy furry ear—
The chill cold faith of modern days,
    The faith and creed austere.

Who would not change our dead church creeds,
    Her bishops and her priests,
For the glad ranks of Grecian gods,
    And the glad Grecian feasts?

Who would not live with thee, dear youth,
    And watch the gentle strife
Within thy form that ever stirs
    Of thy sweet twofold life?

Where blends the animal with man,
    The sweet wild woodland grace
Of nature, with the dearer dawn
    Of manhood in thy face.

Then take me from this world grown old,
  And from these days of ours,
To wild and wood and breezy wold,
  And Faun-like forest hours.

GRAVES AT FLORENCE.

Florence, fair Florence, thee I envy not,
  Nor grudge one charm of thine ;
Of all fair Europe fairest spot
  Of earth, and most divine.

Keep, keep thy fair Baptistery, and all
  Thy rich emblazoned streets ;
Each palace with its storied wall,
  That old tradition greets.

Thine old dim Duomo, on whose muffling gloom
  Break Edens of deep red ;
From those rich windows, on whose bloom
  Colour and light are wed.

Thy Tribune, where Love's fevered pilgrims come
  To worship at the shrine
Of her whom e'en our Christendom
  Acknowledges divine.

Keep all thy marble gems—thy sculptured wealth
  Of god and goddess keep ;

And him round whom we come in stealth
  On his most beauteous sleep.

Whose grace so charms, it may not anger us,
  Locked in such soft repose
Of limbs with beauty languorous,
  Of lips sweet as the rose.

Keep these and thy fair Campanile's grace,
  Too fair for other earth;
No other skies should see its face
  Than those of Giotto's birth.

Thy classic Arno and its beauteous bridge,
  Linking thy quays along;
Fiesole and all the purple ridge
  That won our Milton's song.

Keep all to grace thy purple state, fair queen,
  All art and splendour keep—
All but one acre of thy green,
  Where English singers sleep.

Where lordly Landor's honoured head lies low,
  And lion-heart is still;
Nor music from his lips doth flow,
  The poet's heart to fill.

Where gentle Browning never more her lute
  Shall tune to that grand theme;
Whose thunder pealing, woke ranks mute
  From their inglorious dream.

Till the long streets lived out line after line,
　And, marching hand in hand,
The Tuscans fanned the flame divine
　Of freedom through their land.

Freedom's true knights these noble Tuscans were,
　And worthy of her song ;
Whose metred march so stirred them there,
　Thrilling their ranks along.

But now she sleeps her last and songless sleep,
　With Tuscan earth above ;
And Florence doth her relics keep,
　Who, living, won her love.

And these two graves I grudge to thee, O queen,
　Of all thy state ; but these
Few feet of earth that should have been
　O'erwatched by English trees.

A WEDDING.

April, 1867.

I saw her in the old church kneel,
　Upon that first spring morn ;
The April came to give her smiles,
　The sunlight to adorn.

First morn that winter's lingering car
    Rolled off on sluggish wheels,
And bade fair April's earliest smile
    Melt March's icy seals.

She knelt, and through the painted pane
    The sun stole on the fold,
And wimple of her radiant hair,
    The gift of gold to gold.

There rosebud charm of childhood came
    With girlhood's opening grace,
As, glimmering up the old church aisle,
    Eight maidens took their place.

There Helen and her sister Maud,
    Scarce sharing twenty years,
Hid, blushing, 'midst the ripe rose ranks
    Of girls amid their peers.

There Marion knelt, and Margaret,
    And radiant Gwendolyne,
And Lady Alice, and the rose
    Of all the eight—Claudine.

But fairer still, queen-rose of all,
    Was she who softly spoke
The words that seemed to gently twine
    'Midst his as vine round oak.

His manly accents rose in strength
    From the stout Scottish heart,

And e'er they died, the rhythmic flow
    Of hers took up their part.

Like river in full-volumed strength,
    He poured his hearty speech ;
Like rill that runneth through the reeds,
    In haste that stream to reach,

She seemed to haste to melt her life
    In his for evermore,
So swiftly chimed her answering vow
    To every vow he swore.

The Scottish Doric gave its *verve*
    In him in each stout word ;
The Southern Saxon's sweeter note
    In each response was heard.

So go they forth, and in a world
    Where half is epicene,
May he of manhood be the lord,
    And she of woman queen !

CLAUDINE.

Look up, and let me see the peace
    Of eyes serene,
'Neath hair drawn back in nut-brown fleece
    From brow, Claudine.

What far-famed faces long ago
   Have I thus seen,
Full front me with such brow of snow
   From frames, Claudine.

The painters of proud periods past
   Have matched your mien,
And many a canvas caught you fair
   And fast, Claudine.

Bright snowy brow, bright lifted up,
   White gloss and sheen ;
And lips that might be angels' cup,
   To sip, Claudine.

So tenderly all woman's wiles
   Seem mixed therein,
As though all epochs lent their smiles
   To bless Claudine.

The heavens' child to them you were,
   One hard to wean ;
They loved and would have kept you there,
   Their own Claudine.

But God took pity on the earth,
   So poor and mean ;
And sent it pattern of fresh worth,
   In thee, Claudine.

As earth's new Eve He thee hath sent,
　Since Adam's sin ;
In every age with woman's, blent
　Thy soul, Claudine.

It shone in beauty, love, and truth,
　By Boaz seen ;
And made the beauteous gleaner, Ruth,
　His bride, Claudine.

It dwelt in Jephtha's daughter, when,
　With brow serene,
She bent to death as thou again
　Would'st do, Claudine.

Thou would'st resign thy life e'en now,
　Of seventeen,
To help thy father keep such vow
　As his, Claudine.

This was in Israel, but in Greece
　Was sister seen
To dig a grave, then go in peace
　To hers, Claudine.

In Aulis, when all wind had ceased,
　Fair Iphigene
Came meekly to the votive priest
　To die, Claudine.

A strong man doubting seems to fear
 The sword's point keen,
His wife beholding, sheds no tear,
 Nor shrinks, Claudine.

But falling on the point, she cried,
 With smiling mien,
" Pætus, it hurts not," thus Arria died
 A Greek Claudine.

To live again and bless the earth
 In every scene,
Where legend blows of woman's worth
 And love, Claudine.

In every country knighthood's lance
 Has made thee queen ;
And Spain, and Italy, and France,
 Have their Claudine.

But most our England, where, in times
 Swept from us clean,
You ruled the poets' hearts and rhymes
 For good, Claudine.

Whose verse raised not as one has now,
 Hymn to Faustine ;
But mirrored Unas pure as snow,
 Or thou, Claudine.

Or meek Griseldas, or the grace
  Of Imogen,
That dawns to-day from Faucit's face
  And thine, Claudine.

Or Lear's Cordelia, or the spring's
  Bright Rosaline,
Whose laugh still Arden over rings
  With mirth, Claudine.

Or the bluff king's bright second wife,
  Fair young Boleyne,
Whose slender neck, marred by the knife,
  Matched thine, Claudine.

Or Dudley's Jane set in her hair,
  Poor ten days' queen,
A crown, not that she was to wear
  For aye, Claudine.

All these were shrines and temples made
  To set therein
That spirit which to-day is laid
  On thee, Claudine.

On this sweet time of gracious hours,
  And hearts wherein
Christ lives, this Christian time of ours,
  Smiles sweet Claudine.

If one should kneel and worship you,
  He would not sin,
But be God's own more truly through
  Such love, Claudine.

And should'st thou love him back again,
  Thy love I ween,
Would crown a slave the king of men,
  Thy slave, Claudine.*

LINES IN CEMETERIES.

COMPOSED IN THE GLASGOW CEMETERY.

How different from the hurrying tread
  Where other bridges are,
The silent steps that cross thy bridge
  And stream, Molendinar!

* In these lines to "Claudine," the imitation of Mr. Swinburne's
fine poem "Faustine" is obvious and intentional, my object being,
while I employ the same metre, and in some instances even the same
phrases, to teach a lesson the very opposite of that taught in
"Faustine." I may add that Claudine is really the name of the
young lady whose peculiar beauty, so pervaded with reminiscence
of old pictures, especially the pictures of Sir Joshua Reynolds, sug-
gested to me this imitation or reversal of Mr. Swinburne's poem.

Their arches join with happy link
  The shores with labour rife;
From this sad shore of Lethe falls
  Each wave of human life.

There men are rushing on in haste
  To meet their fellow-men;
Here mourners leave the one pale form
  They ne'er shall meet again.

How oft in other lands I've seen,
  In many a wistful dream,
The vision of that single arch
  Which spans thy sullen stream;

From terrace height to terrace height,
  Have seen each funeral street
Run down, till gravestones on the hill
  The valley gravestones meet;

And thinking on the hallowed earth,
  That lies so thickly here,
The Scottish faith more holy seemed,
  The Scottish land more dear.

And now, when seven years have fled,
  I gaze on them again,
The pillared paths upon the hill,
  The river, and the glen.

Here merchant, actor, preacher lie,
  Where all may safely sleep;

O'er all the blue arch bends alike,
　　Alike the earth will keep.

The living city widens on,
　　Afar its mansions spread,
So, silently from year to year,
　　This city of the dead.

The merchant city leaning down,
　　Seems still, with kindly care,
From many a thronging street to watch
　　And guard the sleepers there.

And so, I greet thee once again,
　　Though seven years have fled
Since last I crossed thy solemn bridge,
　　To muse upon thy dead.

I scarcely note their loss, and yet
　　What happy days they close !
What other seven years to me
　　Shall bring the bliss of those ?

The fairest, richest ones of all
　　Man's threescore years and ten,
The music of their merry march
　　Life will not play again.

Life's music never more for me
　　Such jocund notes will sound ;
Henceforth, with less of drum and trump
　　I pass less sunlit ground.

Adventure scarce will have the charm
    It had in those bright years;
Romance will hardly win from me
    The same delicious tears.

Fled are those swift alternate moods
    That cross life's April morn;
The diamond moments of delight,
    From dismal moments born.

More calm, more even beats my pulse,
    That scarce again will bound
With rapture at some snowdrop seen,
    The first above the ground.

The yellow cowslip on the lawn,
    And many a daffodil
Will dance as gaily in the breeze,
    And fringe the babbling rill;

And they to me will tell more plain
    Than any preacher's lore—
Ay, plainer than the tombstones here,—
    My April days are o'er.

It is not that I love them less,
    Or that they are less bright;
But, springing side by side with them,
    Sad memories dim my sight.

I cannot grasp them as I did,
    The future all unknown;

And Innocence and Hope with me
   False prophets that have flown.

Ah! how these thoughts come thronging now,
   As here I rest awhile,
And think this day, on life's short chart
   Has marked another mile.

My birthday! graves around me lie,
   And many a grave beside,
Of hopes long buried in my heart,
   Dead love and perished pride.

Oh! wheels of hope long, long run down,
   Oh! springs of love now dried;
What should I wish for but a grave
   'Midst those I stand beside?

IN A MILITARY CEMETERY.

I wandered out beyond the town,
   And then a sudden turn
Led me to where the ground was marked
   With many a funeral urn.

A crowded graveyard, where no grave
   Swelled a few years ago;
Yet now the tombstones flag it o'er,
   And line it row by row.

I paused not by the sculptured urns,
  That stood in separate pride,
But passed to where the humbler dead
  Were lying side by side.

The dull grey walls ran coldly round,
  The dull, grey church at hand;
A dreary stillness lay o'er all
  That sad and silent land,

Where lay the hearts that once had beat
  So loud with life and lust;
The wild, brave hearts, that moulder now
  So calmly in the dust.

Oh! brave ones who have breasted round
  Our land from every foe;
Cold are the limbs the scarlet once
  Wrapped with its martial glow.

How reckless were your manly lives,
  Earth's prodigals ye were;
Wild spendthrifts of youth, health, and strength,
  God bless ye lying there!

God look with love where, in their shrouds,
  Mere boys have gone to sleep;
Oh! tightening heartstrings, would that ye
  Would loose and let me weep!

I turned away, my heart was sick—
  Too sick for sob or tear;

Oh! youthful heart, oh! youthful hope,
    Lying so silent here—

Oh! valiant men, oh! gallant race,
    That buckler us from ill,
God guard ye in your careless lives,
    God save ye lying still!

A PICTURE.

NARCISSUS TO LUCILE.

THE spring gives way—the lid flies back—
    And once again I gaze
On that dear face, so wildly loved
    In those long-perished days

Of youth and hope, whose purple flush
    O'er every prospect lay,
Showed all life's roses, but concealed
    The dreary after way.

Dear face, how much of joy comes back,
    As dimly through my tears,
I gaze on thee and summon up
    The tale of those wild years.

My fair Lucile, whom first I met
    Within the Tuscan land,
There first gazed on thy gentle eyes,
    And clasped thy loving hand.

Thy face smiles on me from the past,
    With mild and tender grace ;
O God! what would I give once more
    To see that worshipt face?

It may be that I wronged thee, love,
    In hot and sudden haste,
And crushed a heart that held till then
    For me Love's white rose chaste.

But even wert thou false, as I,
    Half maddened, then believed,
I would the past could be again,
    And I again deceived.

O! could I clasp thee now as then,
    Though guilt be in thy heart,
It should beat still on mine, Lucile,
    Beat nevermore to part.

I would heap all thy faults on mine,
    And bear the double share ;
For, O! thy sins were easier borne
    Than this, my lone despair.

A REVERIE.

LUCILE TO NARCISSUS.

WHEN over the ridge of the Pitti roofs,
 The rose lights are swooning to white,
And the evening grey takes a sterner hue,
 Ere it melt in the purple of night;

How lonely I sit in my chamber then,
 As the twilight gathers around;
And the dim damp mist of the dying day
 Stealeth swift from the dark'ning ground.

How lonely recalling the dead hours, when
 All my world lay within its walls;
Lie silent, my heart, why that bitter cry?
 He is far from thy passionate calls.

Nay, cry not; nay, cry not, he cannot hear,
 Miles and rivers between us lying;
And my ears vainly strain through the hush of night
 For a whisper of his replying.

Now my pulse beats faint, and my heart sinks low,
 For the hour comes swiftly along,
When the sound of his step came as music to me,
 And the sound of his voice as a song.

I will cheat myself of my anguish awhile,
 I will whisper he's near, he's near;

I will watch the hands as they creep o'er the clock,
　To the moment that brought him here.

If now I should hear his step on the stairs,
　If now hear his knock at the door,
How my life would leap into fairy land,
　Where my fancies have run before!

O! my king and my idol, my heart's own love,
　Are these fancies idle and vain ;
Shall my heart leap up at thy knock no more
　With a joy that is sharper than pain ?

Shall the violet breath from thy presence blown,
　Stream no more on my chamber's air;
Nor the night blaze out with a sudden light,
　As it feels thou hast entered there ?

It may be that never again I shall hear
　Nearing sound of thy welcome tread ;
It may be my heart shall spring up no more
　'Twixt to-day and the day I am dead.

It may be that long, long years are to pass,
　That my youth shall be turned to age,
Ere my eyes shall meet thine, that have gazed so oft
　With mine on the poet's page.

Ah! the tender light of those eyes last night
　Was dimmed 'neath the mist of thy tears,
And thy cheek to a paler marble turned
　As I whispered these sudden fears.

And your kisses dwell where you rained them yet,
    Through the rain of your passionate tears;
And I love thee, I love thee, my own dear love,
    With the strength of a thousand years.

With the strength of a thousand years that has bloomed
    Like the wondrous plant in a night,
All my life has blossomed to love for thee,
    My love and my idol, my light!

I named thee Narcissus in fancy's freak,
    And the frolic of those glad hours,
When we stood by the stream in the sweet spring-
       time,
    In the time of Narcissus flowers.

Narcissus! and still I whisper the name,
    And its sound has a magical tone,
And falls like a kiss from my murmuring lips,
    Narcissus, Narcissus, mine own!

Thou wilt come to me, love, from thy Northern clime,
    With the spring's white Narcissus flowers;
And the snowier love of thy stainless heart
    Shall be mine through all future hours.

I will cherish the hope with a rapture, pressed
    To the heart that is thine alone;
I shall see thee return in the sweet spring-time,
    Narcissus, Narcissus, mine own!

THE FELON'S BRIDE.

I saw him steal from the gambling-rooms,
  Weary, and worn, and pale,
With a story writ on his marble face,—
  Was it only a gambler's tale ?

O! more, 'twas the tale of a life begun
  In glory, and pride, and fame,
And then cut short by one maddened act,
  And stained with a felon's shame.

In the flush of his spring, in the dawn of his youth,
  A lad of but eighteen years,
He had blotted his name and erased it for aye
  From the list of his social peers.

One effort was made by his father's pride
  To save him the last disgrace
Of the punishment due to his guilty deed,
  And from taking the convict's place.

And then he was banned from that father's house,
  And barred from the English land—
An exile, an outcast, as much as he'd been
  Sent to herd with the convict band.

'Twas then that we met in those German rooms,
  That all known I still called him friend ;
For the mystic light of his eyes drew mine,
  And my soul seemed with his to blend ;

And I raised him up from his dark despair,
　And I poured in his soul new life;
And at last when I saw that he dared not speak,
　I told him I'd be his wife.

Yes! I know all I lost when I shared his lot,
　Halls and parks in fair English counties;
All the state and pride of an English wife,
　Her duties, and pleasures, and bounties.

But what are these when weighed in the scale
　With the love that my life has blest,
And my husband's smile that lights up for me
　Our happier home in the West—

Where my Gilbert's name is a tower of strength,
　And I think with a passionate pride
Of the noble nature I saved from despair
　By becoming the felon's bride?

A FANCY.

On receiving a White Rose in a Letter.

DEAR LOVE, the fair white rose you send
　Once reddened on your cheek,
Till tears washed all its bloom away,
　And blanched its crimson streak.

But, ah! to me 'tis dearer far,
  A sweeter, lovelier thing,
Than Flora's reddest roses are
  When summer kisses spring.

And but one blossom I could prize,
  And hold more dear than this;
O give it to my eager eyes,
  And to my ardent kiss.

My Marguerite,* thou still art queen
  Of all the flowers on earth,
None other equals thee, I ween,
  No rose has half thy worth.

----------------- --

THE SISTERS.

I KNEW that her brow was nobler,
  And purer and fairer than mine;
But in brilliant ball-rooms where cavaliers gathered,
  I was ever the first to shine.

I was ever the first to be chosen
  As a partner for the dance;
And oft I have glanced at her sitting
  With a heartless scorn in my glance.

* The French daisy.

But an hour struck when the triumphs
    Of the ball-room world grew dim;
And I would have died to win what she won,
    And to be loved by him.

And even then was the victory mine,
    For I stole his heart away;
And my bridesmaid's hand was cold, and her cheek
    Was white on my wedding-day.

But my triumph passed, for he woke from his dream,
    To loathe me, and sicken and die,
And to meet her and love her in heaven above,
    As they love in eternity.

So we each had a kingdom on earth below,
    Each was given a realm of her own;
And to her was the priceless crown of love,
    And to me was the Beauty's throne.

But my kingdom has long in the dust been laid,
    While her reign has commenced above;
And to me is the gnawing of ceaseless regret,
    And to her the undying love;

And to me was the wife's proud lot on earth,
    And to her was the maiden's given;
Now mine is for ever the lonely lot,
    And she is his bride in heaven.

THE WHITE CAPS.

In Upsala, pleasant city,
    Of the Scandinavian land,
Ever gay with song and ditty
    Of its jovial student band;

Not the Bonn boys loudly singing
    Praises of their rushing Rhine,
Nor the Foxes' chorus ringing,
    Wild o'er after-dinner wine,

Sound more blithely through the night-time
    Than these White Caps' serenades
Sung at midnight—that's the right time,
    To the fair Upsalan maids.

Met a troop of merry White Caps
    In this rare old Swedish city,
Cracking joke and jest—mayhaps
    More lighthearted words than witty.

Came, then, towards them, churchwards going,
    An Upsalan maiden gracious,
Stepping lightly, scarcely throwing
    Glance upon these youths audacious.

White Cap—rather Mad Cap, was he,
    Who looked round, and laughing said—
"Certes that fair maid will kiss me,
    Certes that fair maid I'll wed."

He, a poor Upsala student,
  She a maid of high degree;
Hear his comrades check him prudent,
  But one laughs—"I wager free

"Ten score of dollars thou wilt falter
  At the thought of love and her,
When I name the stately daughter
  Of Upsala's governor."

Ten score dollars, they would free him
  Ever more from debt and danger,
Let his widowed mother see him
  Great and famous—stept the stranger—

Stept this White Cap, gaily forward,
  And straightway accosting said—
"I am the poor student, Arvid,
  If thou wilt, my fortune's made.

"Shouldst thou now, a moment casting
  Pride of rank and place aside,
Kiss me, thou wilt give me lasting
  Fortune, honour, fame, and pride."

Paused the maiden, timid glancing
  At the handsome glowing face,
Then her own to his advancing,
  Kissed him with a queenly grace—

Kissed him as she might a brother;
  But the moment his lips pressed hers,

Feelings rose he could not smother,
    And her glowing cheek confest hers.

" I will love that student ever,"
    She unceasing henceforth said—
" I will marry never, never,
    Should I not that student wed."

Then the maiden's father had him
    To the castle brought at last,
In the council-chamber bade him
    Tell the tale of what had past.

Then the father's heart appraised him
    Worthy of his daughter's hand;
And his wager won has raised him
    'Midst the noblest of the land.

THE TWO CECILES.

1.—*The Meeting.*

LET me still recall that meeting,
    At a Lyon's table-d'hôte;
How my eyes ran ever greeting
The fair vision—dishes fleeting
    From the soup to the compôtes.

N

Fair among the foreign faces,
    With its flow of golden curls,
Often still my fancy raises
'Midst some throng in festive places,
    Face and form like that bright girl's.

But one glance, and she had caught me,
    Chained me, held me bound to her;
Vainly active waiters brought me
Plâts, the Lyon's carte had taught me,
    Did to English tastes defer.

I could feast but on her beauty,
    From the first dish to the last;
Vainly waiters did their duty,
Potage, poisson, legumes, rôti,
    Were but glanced at, and then past.

Through the courses gazing on her,
    I could but her graces note;
How the subtle light o'ershone her,
Of the gold hair left to wander
    Rippling round her slender throat;

How the room seemed to remind her,
    With a girl's fresh glad surprise,
That the scenes of home behind her,
She at last had lived to find her
    'Neath a foreign city's skies.

Such her timid sweet confusion,
  Such her bright instinctive grace,
That I half think some delusion,
Some fair spirit-world illusion
  Brought before me that fair face.

With the gold curls wandering round it,
  Falling in a bright confusion,
As some ribbon that had bound it,
Fluttering downwards half unwound it
  From her hair's unchecked profusion.

Somewhat careless, too, the wrapping
  Of the snowy muslin's shade,
And some clasp or button snapping,
Lent new grace in the mishapping,
  To the arm it half betrayed.

All was graceful, soft, and artless
  In her girlish, gentle guise;
E'en the stoic—cynic—heartless,
Well I know him, near me startles,
  Lest he melt 'neath those sweet eyes.

All my heart in worship rose,
  Melted and then madly burned:
That of all the speechless vows
My fond gazing must disclose,
  I might have but one returned.

N 2

Well, her father sitting next her,
    With Time's frost upon his head,
Whose cold bearing doubtless vex'd her,
Whose cold glance must have perplex'd her,
    Through the sunny life she led,

Never noticed my eyes gazing,
    On his dinner deep intent ;
Seldom his proud eyelids raising,
Frigidly each dish appraising,
    As the courses came and went.

When they rose, the dinner ending,
    I rose swiftly with them, too,
Some hope with my madness blending,
To arrest her footsteps tending
    Where my steps might not pursue.

Soft her snowy muslin's flowing,
    Sweeps the ground in graceful folds,
Glides she onwards rapid going,
When some nail from boards upgrowing
    Takes her dress and tightly holds.

While her footsteps still advancing,
    Call me Goth or call me Vandal ;
Fixed my eyes to their entrancing,
On the fair foot forward glancing,
    Thin kid shoe and classic sandal.

I sprang forward to unloose her,
  Swift the robe from nail unbound;
Then, not wishing to confuse her,
As I drew back sad to lose her,
  Saw her kerchief on the ground.

She had passed with footstep fleeter,
  When the slight delay was o'er,
I must keep it till I meet her,
And with this excuse to greet her,
  Will the handkerchief restore.

To my lips I fondly pressed it,
  Sweeter far than rose's scent;
Tenderly my mouth carest it,
In my prayers ten times I blest it,
  For the hopes that from it went.

And to-day my desk o'erhauling,
  With an eager rapid search, if
I could find for some one calling
Some old letter—my eyes falling,
  Met again that treasured kerchief.

Lifting from my desk's recess,
  I that relic gently feel;
To my lips again I press,
The six letters I still bless,
  The six letters of " Cecile."

And the kerchief still there lying,
　Tells the tale that I would tell;
June-tides and Decembers dying,
May-tides, winters coming, flying,
　How that meeting ne'er befel.

For that eve, not faded quite,
　With the mail a letter brought me;
Told me travelling day and night,
On my backward, homeward flight,
　To reach him who dying sought me.

I might yet his roof-tree gaining,
　To my father's heart still press me;
Greet his eyes still fondly straining,
Hear the old man's accents waning,
　Strengthen still that they might bless me.

*　　　*　　　*　　　*　　　*　　　*

Sought I then those bright eyes glancing,
　Searching Europe vainly o'er,
For the blissful moment's chancing,
When with happy steps advancing,
　I that kerchief might restore.

But in vain sought late and early,
　For the chance that might reveal;
By the autumn's vine-clad Lurlei,
Through Norwegian landscapes surly,
　The fair form of my Cecile.

Five years fleeting in that search, if
  Time to me would yet reveal
Her to whom belonged the kerchief,
Her whom still I fondly worship,
  My life's loved and lost Cecile.

My old hall and chace foregoing,
  Wandering still afar from home,
Went I one spring morn, o'erflowing
With the wealth of violets growing,
  To see Keats' grave near Rome.

Cast beneath a white cross rising,
  Near that grave a figure knelt;
Ere it rose at the apprising,
Of my sudden steps surprising,
  All the truth my instinct felt.

I felt all at one swift glancing,
  Ere the old man had withdrawn him;
And my heart's wild tumult dancing,
Drew me on like one advancing
  'Gainst the fates that vainly warn him.

In the March sun brightly streaming,
  Read the words its rays reveal;
There upon the white cross gleaming,
Read the end of my life's dreaming,
  " Sacred to our dear Cecile."

Seen an hour, loved for ever,
  I was but a boy in years;
But no lapse of years could sever,
And from my heart will fade never,
  The one image it enspheres.

Seen and loved, and unpossessed,
  Still her vision haunting;
All the lips that mine have blest,
All the hands my hands have prest,
  Still leave something wanting.

Beauteous vision, since I met her,
  All my May of life has fled;
Still my heart cannot forget her,
Still my fancies fondly set her
  Where her fate has never led.

Five-and-twenty years have blossomed,
  Faded, died, and gone since then;
And were all my care and cross summed,
All my life's mishap and loss summed,
  They indeed would wear my pen.

I was then a lad of twenty,
  Rich and free to choose a wife;
Maidens I might wed in plenty,
All passed over questioned " meant he
  To prefer a single life."

All their arts were vain to lure me,
  For my heart was true as steel;
But one image could allure me,
One of matchless grace and purity,
  The bright image of Cecile.

Ah! my friend, how I still love her,
  Let my life's long story tell;
How that earth of Rome doth cover
All my dream of love close over,
  Where my heart shall ever dwell.

Take the story as I write it,
  From this German town's hotel;
For I think as I indite it,
One friend, though he ne'er can right it,
  Will its pathos feel full well.

2.—*The Marriage.*

A month since, my friend, in writing
  My life's story sadly summing;
When that tale in grief inditing,
Of my early love's swift blighting,
  Little knew I what was coming.

How that eve my chair in taking,
  At the Munich table-d'hôte,
Sudden from the past awaking,
Like a sun from dark clouds breaking,
  Gold hair rippling round her throat,

Sat in youth and beauty beaming,
  Sat in gentle girlish guise ;
Such as first upon me gleaming,
Shot through all my life one dreaming,
  Cecile met my youthful eyes.

Surely, surely, Heaven sent her,
  Surely, surely, angels brought her—
Her in whom my life doth centre,
She who with her mother's blent her
  Own bright beauty—Cecile's daughter.

I, though twenty years her elder,
  Still have won that fresh young heart,
And my age has not repelled her,
And this morn my arms have held her,
  Folded close no more to part.

For this morn beneath the altar,
  She with gentle grace did kneel ;
And in saying o'er Love's psalter,
Scarcely once her lips did falter,
  Till she rose my wife, Cecile.

SONG.

No more, no more shall thy kisses rain
  Like the rose-rain fast and sweet ;
Would God they had kissed my life away,
  Would God I lay dead at thy feet !

I should not have lived to part with thee thus,
  I should not have seen the day
When the silence of death would be better far
  Than thy footsteps passing away.

And oh that my sun of life could set
  With yon sun now low in the west,
With the last light faded from my life,
  With the last hope dead in my breast ;
Would God that the thread of my life might break,
  Ere the break of another day !
And oh that I might fall dead, my love,
  When thy footsteps have passed away !

For I have loved in my light, light youth,
  And have listened, ah, well-a-day,
To the echoes of many a pleasant step,
  As they passed from my life away ;
But oh how feeble such old loves seem,
  How light in the scales they weigh,
With the love that has followed thee night by night,
  As thy footsteps faded away !

And now we must part when the whole, whole world,
  And my heart and my soul are in thee ;
Oh that I had died in my childhood's years,
  Ere I knew what such love could be ;
Now, when all's over, and said and done,
  What remains to my dying day,
But the sound in my ears, like the clay on the dead,
  Of thy footsteps passing away ?

COUSIN CLARE; OR, MY BROTHER'S WIFE.

How like this Christmas Eve to one long gone,
Whose torches, now through mists of ten dead years,
I still see shining as they shone that night,
When she from falling snow and outward gloom,
Slid swiftly into ruddy rays, that shot
Glad welcome from the huge yule log, whose heart
Had hoarded the fierce flame close to its core,
Till smote by Roger's sturdy arm, it sprang
From every vein and crimsoned all the hall,
And rained its redness on the close-clad form
Of her who hastened swiftly in, as though
Behind her lay a world all gloom and chill;
Before her, light, and love, and friends.   'Twas thus
That Christmas Eve came Cousin Clare to us —
To the old Grange and us came Cousin Clare—
The dear old Grange where I and Arthur lived,
With none to check us or control our will;
For he who might have done so, more a boy
In heart than we, lived out his liberal life
In letting all around him have their way;
But, most of all, his boys, to whom he felt
No love could make amends for loss of hers
Who died in giving me and Arthur birth,
For we were twins, though I, the elder born,
Was heir to the fair fertile acres farmed
For some six miles around our ancient hall;
And being twins, men marvelled much that we

Were shaped and fashioned on such different plan ;
For, save that both were dark in hair and eyes,
And held some trick or gesture of our race
In common, as the slight soft slur which some
Called silver-toned in sliding o'er an R,
We differed else as they of different blood,
For Arthur bore two inches over me,
And far outspanned me in his breadth of chest ;
The rose of richer manhood flushed his cheek,
A fuller flame of life fed all his frame,
And beauty, made more beautiful by these,
Gave all its gloss and glory to his youth.
He would have been the warrior, I the clerk
In olden times—I had the clerk's pale cheek
And student nature, loving rather lore
Of book and ancient manuscript than all
The riot pasturing round my brother's life ;
No question which the nobler, he or I ;
As well compare King Arthur with poor Pope,
The pearl of paladins with peevish Pope ;
Or Paris, leaping to his Helen's bed,
With Chatterton on his lone pallet laid ;
Or sweep and swing of coronation pomp,
With the dead pauper's pinched funereal train ;
Or the earth-echoing cheer at Lucknow heard,
With the child's piping on a thin-tongued reed ;
Or anything that's grand, and glad, and glorious,
With anything that's wan, and worn, and weak.

As Arthur's lusty life and lordly laugh,
With Leonard's listless pace and languid mien;
But differing thus in two things we agreed,
Each held his brother to his heart of hearts,
And each was loyal knight to Cousin Clare.
How glad the old Grange grew once she had come,
How all its chambers seemed to own a spell—
The subtle spell of gentle girlhood's grace
Shed from the roses of her fifteen years!
Three years had come and died, and still with us
Lived Cousin Clare, and now the blushing bud
Of girlhood's opening bloom had filled and rounded
To the rich orb that rings a warmer charm,
When a swift change crept o'er her summer life;
Like a light shadow on a sunlit lake,
A shadow seemed to tremble o'er her face,
Then melt in smiles to waver back again,
Came faltering tones instead of frank clear words,
And drooping eyes in place of clear frank looks;
Half feared I to interpret what my heart
Yet whispered might be stored of bliss for me.
That I loved Clare I felt full well; that she
Could love or think of me, I had not dreamt
Till now, when those down-drooping lids told more
Than speech, and sudden blush than words told more.
O now my life seemed caught up from the earth;
And, lifted on a thousand fluttering wings
Of fresh-fledged hopes, delicious days danced on,

While breeze from fairyland blew on my brow,
And I could catch the cheer of Elfin horns ;
While rose my heart full strung to love's glad song,
And all the present chimed with tones of love,
And all the future wore love's golden glow.
But still I hived my rapture, fearing yet
To speak, lest words should break the fairy spell,
And I should see dissolve and melt away
This glittering fabric of a lover's dream.
O, fools, who trifle thus with time and chance,
And let the moments nought can e'er reclaim
Lapse by, who see the tide that rises once
For every man full in, and feel the breeze
Blow fresh, yet slumber on the shores of life,
Then wake to find that they are left forlorn
Upon a barren land, while far and faint
From o'er the distant ocean comes the cheer
Of comrades sailing on to happy isles !
While lingering thus one summer morn I heard
My brother say—" Come, Leonard, come and walk
Across the park with me, and hear a secret
I shall tell the first to you." He jocund
Took my arm, and we went into sun-shine
Of the rich June-tide, and June was golden
In my heart that morn, nor wrapt the landscape
In a warmer drowse of summer peace, nor drew
The swarming bees in thicker clusters round
The lime-tree blossoms, than this June of life

Enwrapt me in its fervent folds, and nursed
A swarm of happy thoughts that clustered still
Round the rich central fancy of my heart.
Then Arthur spoke, and woke me from my dream,
Half laughing—laughter leaping 'neath his tones—
Laughter on whose light silver flood his words
Flowed down like ingots from his heart's rich gold,
But fell on mine with weight of iron bars :—
"Leonard, you know, at least, I think have guessed,
I long have loved our cousin, and this morn
I asked her would she marry me?" "And she?"
"Of course said, 'yes,' or else I would not thus
Have brought you out to hear. Well, wish me joy ;
Or, think you, Clare has thrown herself away?
I own I am not worthy of her ; you,.
Dear Leonard—you, whose mind can mate with hers,
Methinks were fitter far for Cousin Clare
Than is the graceless madcap who has won her ;
But you care not for woman's love. To you
A musty book is prize more valued far
Than 'the white wonder of a Juliet's hand.' "
So careless bantered he, while I—well, I,
Struck cold as though December's frost had ta'en
All summer from my days, made answer thus :—
"O, surely you are worthy of her love—
Of any woman's love—were it alone
For your fair inches and your great wide chest,
Your strength, your daring, and your handsome face ;

'Tis men like you alone are made to win
A lady's love; and, for my part, I think
Those women right who choose a man by inches;
Not for his mental height, those right who weigh
Him in the scales as worth so many stone,
Made a few ounces more or less by weight
Of brain." Thus far I spoke in bitter scorn ;
Then sudden changing, cried—" God bless you both,
Dear Arthur, you and Cousin Clare, for she
Not worthier is than you ; worthy of her,
True knight, and brave as Arthur was of old,
So is this Arthur whom I brother call ;
Yes, you are worthy of a lady's love ;
But not alone for your fair stature's height,
Nor great wide chest, but for your heart as wide,
Where she who dwells, dwells in a golden house."
So pelted him with words of praise that he,
Confused and blushing, might not look on me.
And they were wed—were wed and gone, thank God !
And I might nurse my grief, the saddest heir
To riches all the country round.
                    Two years
Crept on. From Arthur I had often had
Bright, cheerful letters; he and Clare were still
Glad wanderers over Europe, seeing all
The glories of the old Italian towns ;
And I—my father in his grave—still dwelt
Alone, and nursed my hidden grief the more ;

o

And as the 'plaining plover wheeleth round,
Where, 'midst the rushes, lies her wounded mate,
All heedless of the hovering hawk above,
So wheeled I round the haunts of Cousin Clare,
While o'er me flapped Despair expectant wings,
Waiting to glut its beak within my heart,
And the two years gone by, as twenty seemed,
So ploughed they furrows on my cheek and brow;
Faded was now my feeble flower of youth,
And all life looked one dull December day;
When, lo! the storm broke suddenly.

                  One morn
A servant entering with a thin, clasped volume
In his hand, told me that workmen making
Some repairs, had, in the room where Clare had slept,
Displaced an escritoire, and niched behind it
Lay this volume, which he straightway brought to me.
It was in manuscript, the writing Clare's;
And there, 'midst tendrils of the sweet girl hand,
Were set the rubies of her matchless mind
In diary kept till near her wedding-day;
And still the writing lured me on and on,
And, half unconscious that I read, I read,
Till from one page the truth like lightning leaped,
And scorcht me where I stood.

                Now all was known—
All what?—that Clare had loved me all along;
And here the whole sad tale of wretchedness,

How she had feared her love was half betrayed
To one indifferent, and so, to shield her pride,
And 'scape a life grown misery, life beneath
The roof with one she loved, who guessed her love,
And scorned it, she had shelter sought within
The only haven near—my brother's heart :—
" With Arthur, I shall go afar from home—
Afar from all that links my life to Leonard's ;
'Neath Arthur's smile hope shall revive again,
And gratitude may ripen into love.
Then let this page be now the silent tomb
Of all a girl's wild hopes, lie there dead flowers
Of a love whose blossoms bloomed in vain for him."
O God, and was this true? and were we all
Alike undone by one sick dreamer's fault,
Who dug the grave of others' happiness
While thinking he had hollowed but his own ?
Scarce, with the volume, staggering to my desk,
Had I there locked it safe from prying eyes,
Ere all surged round me, and I lay as dead.
And slowly from that fever woke to find
A sweet, pale face, but sad, bent over me,
And see a shape in widow's garb glide past,
While as from mists of morning smiles the sun,
So gradual through the mist of illness grew
Distinct upon my gaze the face of Cousin Clare ;
Then sudden knew I Arthur dead, as sudden
All was blank again.

Yes, you guess shrewdly;
But little now remains.   Some three years gone
Since Clare and I, in English laws despite,
And the loud censure of our English world,
Were wed in Germany, where now we dwell,
My English acres for a German's farm
Right well exchanged, since here we happy dwell,
'Midst those wide German hearts and ampler minds,
That only laugh to learn our island ban
'Gainst marriage with a brother's wife.   " Some piece
Of priestcraft wedged so tight within your Church,
To drag it out might pull the fabric down."
While we, still closer drawn by that old tie,
Seem still to cherish Arthur's memory more— ·
My own dead brother, who had happy died,
Watched o'er by tender looks of gratitude,
Which ever he mistook for those of love,
And love's best counterfeits and nearer love
From such a heart as Clare's than would be those
Of others, had they coined their life to love.

So ends my tale; let those condemn who list,
So Cousin Clare and I live happy still.

FROM A CLUB-ROOM WINDOW.

VARIOUS landscapes, glowing prospects
    In my wanderings I have seen;
Wild Killarney's purple mountains,
    Windermere in summer sheen,
Niederwald's romantic temple,
    And the Wyndcliff's lovelier view,
Eberstein, near Baden-Baden,
    Rich in Autumn's golden hue.

Edinburgh, Paris, Milan,
    Each has showed her rival charms;
Florence half a captive held me,
    In her soft seductive arms;
But I judge, in sober choosing,
    Not a landscape can compete
With that from the C. S. window,
    Pall Mall and St. James's Street.

But, if sitting in this window,
    I should ask you what you see,
Ten to one, a moment glancing,
    You would careless answer me—
"Sloppy street and winter's sky,
    Rain, confound it, pouring yet,
Muddy men and draggled women,
    All December's dirt and wet.

" Horrid climate this to live in ;
    Why, last year, I can remember
How the Pincian seemed like June-tide
    To the last day of December ;
And in Paris often sitting
    (Ah ! you catch me tripping there)
I forgot that you were with me
    In that winter weather rare.

" When the icy winds seemed snipping
    With old Hiems' sharpest shears,
On the Boulevarts Italiens,
    Little pieces off our ears ;
Still no weather half so bad is—
    Just look down that dismal street—
As our London weather, blank it,
    With its fog, and rain, and sleet."

Yes, I look ; but, to my vision,
    There is neither rain nor sleet,
But a glorious vista stretching
    Down thy hill, St. James's Street—
Down thy hill and round the angle,
    Turning sharp to proud Pall Mall,
Just in front of that Quadrangle,
    Where the Court officials dwell.

"Match me, prospect in the wide world,
    With the prospect now before me,

Where the glittering vista gleameth
    With an age of English story."
Ah! I hear your laughter ringing
    At the wild demand I make—
Laugh ye fresh from Highland heather,
    Moor and forest, hill and lake.

Laugh, I love to hear the laughter,
    Child of harmless fun and mirth;
Not the changeling satire fathered,
    To which scoff has given birth;
Send your arrows ringing round me,
    I will be your willing target;
Let you call me wild, eccentric,
    So your vision will enlarge it.

So that from this club-room window
    You may see, as I see clear,
Form and fashion ever changing
    With the change of time and year;
But your banter rises louder,
    And one wiser than his fellows
Jeers, " We fancy Timbs has told us,
    Sala, too, all you would tell us."

What you kindly fix a limit,
    You will stop at six-score years;
Thanks, 'tis true a longer record
    Gave its vision to our fears;

Ghosts tremendous seemed arising
  From the medieval tomb,
When the Palace was a "spital,"
  And the Park all marsh and gloom.

Fancy had, like Campbell's sunset,
  Learnt experience' mystic lore,
And your wondrous legends coming,
  Cast their shadows on before.
But you'll kindly spare us dating,
  But from the Hogarthian era,
Kinder still if you will take up
  The old tale a little nearer.

Just suppose we say from Brummell,
  Part from "Duncombe's Life" just out,
Tell us in your meagre verses
  Things that we know all about.
Come, old fellow, now be candid,
  Don't you think we've heard enough
Of Pall Mall's "sweet shady side,"
  "Our fat friend," and "all that stuff?"

Joked at thus, I look around me,
  Check my Pegasus in canter,
And dismount a little wiser
  For that sudden douche of banter.
But, dear readers, weigh your losses,
  Weigh them well, and duly greet;

You have lost—why, all my verses—
    Verses on St. James's Street.

Pleasant 'tis from club-room window
    To look out, and who can doubt it?
Dream the olden time is with you,
    So you do not rhyme about it.
But if verses flow upon you,
    Take this short advice and sweet ;
Choose some ground less often trodden,
    Than that of St. James's Street.

ON KISSING THE QUEEN'S HAND.

SMALL marvel that my heart beat quick,
    When first I took thy hand,
And kissed it, bending low before
    Our Lady of the Land.

Queen of the English land art thou,
    A glorious realm, in sooth,
First leader in the glorious march
    Of freedom and of truth.

For this my head in reverence bent,
    For this my knee was bowed ;
For this none brought thee truer heart
    In all that loyal crowd.

For not to me did it seem aught
    That thou wert ruler o'er

The dim barbaric pomp of lands
    Beyond our English shore.

I heard, nor deemed it much to hear,
    That never sun goes down,
But ere its last rays fade from one,
    It gilds another town

Of that vast realm that calls thee Queen;
    But I knelt not for this,
Nor took thy hand and freely gave
    A subject's loyal kiss.

With reverent love my lips I pressed
    Upon that gentle hand,
Because it held the sceptre of
    My own dear English land.

And for that noble German's sake,
    "Mine own ideal knight,"
My heart's true king now gone for aye,
    From mine and England's sight.

Thou uncrowned King, more royal thou,
    By right of simple worth,
Than if, perchance, a triple crown
    Had come to thee by birth.

Sleep soundly in thy knightly grave,
    Our loss is but thy gain;
Oh! mind of worth, oh! heart of gold,
    Oh! wise and thoughtful brain.

EVENING DREAMS.

I SIT in my study at eventide,
  While the shadows around me close,
And the flickering flame, from side to side,
  With a ceaseless motion goes—
With a ceaseless motion touches the walls,
  And their secrets flash to light
For a moment, then swiftly a shadow falls,
  And snatches them into the night.
I sit and I look through the eventide
  At the vision of seven bright years,
Whose fruit is around me on every side,
  As my glance through the dim light peers :
There my pictures hang on the study walls,
  That were bare when first I came ;
There a sudden blaze on the landscape falls,
  And strikes on the golden frame
Of my favourite Cuyp with his glassy stream,
  And his cattle wading knee-deep
In water so tranquil, it seems but a dream
  Of cows that have fallen asleep ;
And I know where the shadows so thickly fall,
  Were the light to suddenly flow,
What a lustre would break from the oaken wall,
  What a golden colour would glow !

There the picture hangs that I hold most divine,
  But the painter diviner still,
E'en in Raphael's home I have turned from his shrine,
  To worship Sir Joshua's skill;
To me it seems his is the kingliest hand
  That on canvas has ever imprest
The image of all that an age and a land
  Have held loveliest, bravest, and best—
A land that still gauges her artists by him,
  His pictures of others the gauge,
An age that was born for the painter to limn,
  As the painter was born for the age;
Not lily that looks into lily's grace,
  Nor roses that bloom on one tree,
Nor pansies that lurk 'neath the hood with twin face,
  Are so mated and matched as he,
With that era borne on a thousand years,
  That a thousand will scarcely efface,
Where Beauty met Beauty as peer meets his peers,
  And grace held the mirror to grace;
Each beauty he stole on his canvas lives still,
  With the charm he alone could bestow,
Though fifty have risen to boast of their skill,
  Twice ten thousand their trumpets to blow,
Yet, though clique and though coterie clustered around
  Their Sherwin, their Cosway, their Lawrence,
As critics to-day Gibson's Venus have found
  To rival the Venus of Florence;

Still, lord of the realm of fair women he rules,
    With a rule of most absolute sway,
Humanity's artist, supreme o'er all schools,
    For ever sublime as to-day.
Thus I muse and I dream with the picture before me.
    Till suddenly ceasing to glimmer,
Swift the firelight falls, and a shadow steals o'er me,
    My vision grows dimmer and dimmer;
Then brightens where fancy has led me away
    From the four study walls that had bound me,
To where I walk freely in light of midday,
    With Sir Joshua's ladies around me,
To where, in the drowse of the noontide sun,
    As it sleeps on the grand old walk,*
The swarm of the Georgian Court has begun
    To tattle the old world talk ;
There is "Hervey the handsome," a bachelor yet,
    Making straight for Miss Mary Lepel,
Watched by Bath and by Chesterfield, who can forget
    Their joint lines on the " Beau and the Belle ?"
And as Hervey glides up with his butterfly air,
    And that grace none could ever excel,
Mark the flutter that stirs all the fans of the fair,
    When he settles on Molly Lepel ;
See Pope, who regards him from eyelids aslant,
    Mark the spite in that venomous eye,
For the birth of his hideous and scandalous taunt
    On " Lord Fanny " you there may descry,

* In Kensington Gardens.

And there " Lady Mary," who gives sting for sting,
   Is aiming her visage and wit,
With each sentence some arrow she sets on the wing,
   And triumphs to see it has hit ;
Poor Miss Howe is the target she aimed at just now,
   And the whisper and titter go round,
'Midst the flutter of fan and the arching of brow,
   That young Lowther has poached on that ground ;
And thus, amid scandal, and gossip, and hints,
   The chat rises louder and louder,
While the air takes a gleam from the silks' tulip tints,
   And a perfume from Maréchale powder.

      So moved they then beneath the trees
        That skirt that glorious walk,
      Which now another century sees,
        And hears a different talk ;
      Where those gay groups once patterned all
        The ground with rich mosaic,
      Now sober Cits' grave footsteps fall,
        In measures most prosaic.
      Where hoop and fan, and patch and hood,
        Each latest *cancan* heard ;
      Where Fashion brought her freshest mood,
        And Wit his wittiest word.
      Now nursemaids wheeling forth their charge,
        Perambulate together ;
      On sordid household themes enlarge,
        Board wages, and the weather.

And still the old elm-trees look down,
　—As they looked long ago,
On courtly groups of George's town,
　Wit, statesmen, belles, and beaux—
And often I, when through the wood,
　My homeward way I'm tracing,
Will linger long in thoughtful mood,
　Beneath their shadows pacing,
Recalling how that morn I went,
　By tracts of well-known land,
Where,—house and grounds in ruin blent,—
　Old Campden used to stand.

CAMPDEN HOUSE.

I wander 'neath thy ancient walls,
　And past their flanking tower;
While memory one by one recalls
　Each pleasant day and hour,

That now have dropt within the crypt
　Of past and vanished pleasures—
The golden days and hours slipt
　Beyond all mortal measures.

O, dark safe crypt, that keeps the hours
　Which never have a fellow—
O, golden days of happy youth,
　No age will ever mellow!

Ye went with me, when first I went,
   A stranger down those ways
That led to Campden House, and lent
   The mansion to my gaze.

When passing through its ancient gates,
   That oped their sculptured screen,
And led to where the winding way
   Was ovalled round the green,

I stood before thee with no dream,
   How often I should stand,
Until few spots on earth could seem
   Familiar as thy land,

I met thy master's face, nor thought
   How often I should meet
The friendly looks it ever brought,
   The kindly words to greet

The stranger in a stranger land,
   Where the old roof uprears
Of Campden House, of Campden House,
   And its three hundred years.

And then the days that came and went,
   And brought me early—late,
At noon or eve, still where the walk
   Would lead to Campden Gate,

To where, beyond the pillared porch,
   Carved with an artist's pride,

With state of old Jacobian days,
  The hall would open wide,

And lead me on to those dear rooms,
  Beneath whose old oak beams,
Some score of friends would battle o'er
A score of madcap schemes.

While play or concert some would vote,
  Some begged a fancy ball ;
Till host and hostess, smiling, asked
  How they could humour all ?

And jesting thus, the light would fade
  From all thine antique bowers,
Their oriel windows helping on
  The gloom of evening hours.

And then the lights would leaping flash
  From twenty score of tapers ;
And fire and candle do their best
  To drive away the vapours.

Each lustre then would grow a heap
  Of molten gold and rubies,
Which, flashing splendour through the rooms,
  Might brighten even boobies,

Were boobies ever on the list,
  Of Campden House set down,
By him who feasted many a year
  The wittiest of the town.

r

O, festal eves at Campden House,
  When gathered round its board;
'Mid jests the viands went their round,
  'Mid jests the wine was poured.

O, festal nights, when, greenroom thronged,
  And actors in their places,
The curtain of thy play-house rose
  To sea of friendly faces!

Which of us thought, when last we saw,
  Beneath thy roof, O friend,
That curtain fall, it should no more
  In Campden House ascend—

That we no more to Campden House
  Should come in merry guise,
That Campden House would never see
  Another summer's skies?

What memories of three hundred years
  Went glimmering past thy doors,
Since first King Jamie's dames and peers
  Trod down thy fresh-laid floors,

To when King Charles's cavaliers,
  To make thy rafters ring,
A jovial crew, one June-tide eve,
  Come riding round their king!

Who sups to-night at Campden House,
  With Campden's new-made lord—

A roystering lot, who drink and sing,
And swear with one accord?

Mayhap they drink and sing the more,
And swear with louder laughters,
To chase the stern Cromwellian hymns
Still clinging round the rafters.

Their jingling sabres die away,
Their plumes shall wave no more;
King Charles is buried twenty years,
King James's reign is o'er;

And Nassau William on the throne,
Rules country, town, and port;
Plants tulip-bulbs at Kensington,
And lays out Hampton Court,

While grown to more majestic state
Than architect did plan,
Old Campden House becomes the Court
Of Stuart Princess Anne.

And all was life and mirth within
Its formal gardens, when
Duke Gloucester, from the tower's tall height,
Reviewed his little men.

But fifty years of change stole on,
'Neath academic rule,
Saw home of peer and princess now,
Become a boarding-school.

Where rosebud forms of slight young girls,
   For sixty years' succession,
Danced lightly o'er the oaken floors,
   In girlhood's gay procession.

Thus year came treading after year,
   And change came fast and faster;
Till saw the house its latest change,
   And owned its latest master.

On Campden House three hundred years
   Wrought memories rich and rare;
One mirk March morn—two hours' fierce flames
   Left ruin brooding there.

Thus I dream and I muse, while the dim moments pass,
   Of that quiet and mystical time;
When fancies flow swift as the sands from the glass,
   And thoughts take the measure of rhyme.
And then pale ghosts of plan on plan,
   Rise up without their acts;
The boy's resolves cry to the man,
   And fancies call to facts.
Bright purposes yet unfulfilled,
   Rich mines still unexplored;
Boy's heart that Time has somewhat chilled,
   Youth's glittering fairy hoard;
And ardent dreams of something great
   And daring to be done;

The working early, working late,
  For fame I never won.
These visions trooping round my chair,
  Like royal Richard's ghosts ;
Will rise when least expected there,
  To plague me with their hosts
Of old-forgotten plans and wishes
  I buried, God knows when ;
But Memory, sometimes too officious,
  Will dig them up again.
Such mood is rare, for where I'm host,
  Content sits as a guest,
Whose favourite motto I love most,
  " All happens for the best."
And all is for the best, my friend,
  'Tis thus we sing together ;
Man's good is still God's destined end,
  Then welcome any weather.
From heaven's four quarters let there go,
  Each season's changing winds ;
And storms of rude discussion blow
  The dust off Tory minds.
Let Bright's reformers arm-in-arm,
  Go walk in dusty legions ;
And Fenians try their every charm
  To fire those fierce Milesians.
For winds and strife alike die off,
  Around our little chamber ;

Which warmer seems for cold and sough,
   And rain of drear December.
And happy spite of all Time thieves,
   And life lets slip away,
I homeward trudge on these raw eves,
   And bless the lucky day
That gave this pleasant niche of home,
   Shut in from all their strife ;
This nook, where faint the voices come,
   Of London's loud-tongued life.
Till all my heart to bursting swells,
   And breaking out at length,
My old, old song, 'mid Christmas bells,
   I sing with all my strength.

A LONDON LYRIC.

Live, London, live, imperial town,
   Thy royal robes spread round,
And sweep them far on every side,
   O'er many a mile of ground.

Grow on for ever—grow in worth,
   And wealth, and power, and pride,
Thou stateliest city of the earth,
   Stretch still on every side.

Throw out new limbs in lusty strength,
   But keep thine ancient heart,

That throbs beyond loud Temple Bar,
  Where thou, old City, art.

The centuries driving on in haste
  Smote fire to thy bones;
The fierce old years have struck a soul
  Into thy solemn stones.

House whispers house throughout the night,
  Each hath its secret story,
They breathe a legend each to each,
  And all grow grey and hoary.

The Roman gave thee strength and state,
  The Saxon mirth and cheer,
The Norman all the glittering pride
  Of prelate, prince, and peer.

The mediæval years have left,
  At every turn and angle,
Their old monastic memories,
  In cloister or quadrangle.

To poets' eyes in place of crowds
  That press round Newgate felons,
Goes the Boy Bishop to St. Paul's,
  The nun to grave St. Helen's.

Far on he looks; and, lo! he sees
  The Tower and its stout warders,
With fair round faces full and fat
  From many Christmas larders.

Oh, live through many a Christmas yet,
    And fatter grow and fatter,
That merry boys may still in jest
    Make query—" Who's your hatter ?"

But looking on ye close, we see
    How change comes fleet and fleeter;
The glittering garb of bluff King Hal,
    Has left the bluff beef-eater.

Thus still the present strips away
    Each shred of old illusion,
And only fairy glamour now
    Can yield such sweet delusion

As stole on me that summer eve,
    When sitting after dinner,
I heard them shout along Cornhill,
    And name the Ascot winner.

I'd rambled long that day among
    A hundred city streets,
Snatching such legends as who roams
    The City ever meets.

A hundred such blew in my face,
    From every coign and angle ;
And swarmed and buzzed within my brain,
    Till all seemed in a tangle.

At last I paused, swung back the doors
    Of S——'s dining-rooms,

Sat down to dine on soup and fish,
    Broiled chicken and mushrooms.

And soup and fish, and chicken done,
    Proof given I could dine—
I, lingering long, quaffed many a glass
    Of old Burgundian wine—

That generous wine, whose nature seems
    Of rare old port to dream,
And that great tipple put aside,
    Ranks first in my esteem.

Then looking out upon Cornhill,
    And all its noise and bustle,
I read the *Standard's* stale remarks
    On Derby and on Russell;

On Hyde Park riots, where we gave
    The roughs enough of rope;
On Gladstone, Bright, and S. G. O.,
    King Victor and the Pope.

And reading thus, my second flask
    Still held a good third part;
When that old wine of Burgundy,
    Seemed stirring all my heart.

'Tis generous wine and sound my host,
    And strikes a noble heat;
I fill and fill again, nor note
    Now how the moments fleet;

For suddenly a change stole o'er
    The eve, the place, the wine;
The room grew quaint, and old, and shrunk,
    The drinking grew divine.

For guests were there with sturdy voice,
    And loud side-shaking laughters,
That echoed round the tavern walls,
    And rolled amid the rafters.

Two hundred years and more slid back,
    Two hundred stirring years;
And Beaumont and Ben Jonson drank
    With Fletcher and his peers.

Cornhill for me revived that eve,
    And wore her ancient glories;
Her famous topers woke once more,
    To wine and witty stories.

Let there be poets still who may
    With me invoke the fairy,
Whose magic wand turns Burgundy
    Or Claret to Canary—

The fairy Fancy, she who rings
    Those after-dinner glasses,
That send us dreaming back to days
    Of Shakespeare's lads and lasses.

For with each added glass I drained,
    The years ran swifter back;

The wine late to Canary turned,
    Was turned again to Sack.

To Sack, indeed, or Malvoisey,
    I hardly could tell which;
Somewhat confused my palate grew,
    But owned the flavour rich.

And places changed as swift as wine,
    From Cornhill to Eastcheap;
I did not walk as other men,
    But went with sudden leap.

I left Ben Jonson drinking still,
    And farther up the ages,
I heard with Falstaff, "Hal," and Poins,
    And such Shaksperian sages.

St. Clement's chimes ring out their tune,
    When swift the scenery changes;
And down the table rows of chairs
    Stand out in formal ranges.

The room another shape assumes,
    Another dress the men,
That fairy hand has plucked me back
    A hundred years again.

That burly form in big arm-chair,
    Who looks a club-room king—
An orb whom satellites surround
    In reverential ring.

'Tis Sam, not Ben, who reigneth now,
    In Hanoverian days;
The one big mouth that soundeth still
    The Stuart monarch's praise.

The strong form rolls, the voice is raised
    Loud over other men;
And still he argues on, although
    None argues back again.

But on my ears his loud-pitched thunder
    Rolls faint and far away;
And the next speech that smites my ear,
    I hear the waiter say—

" Beg pardon, sir, 'tis time to close."
    I start and gaze around,
Rise up, and while I stare about,
    My hat and cane are found.

The bill is paid, the waiter feed,
    And I am in the street,
And pushing on by Ludgate Hill,
    And down the thriving Fleet.

The visions I have dreamed depart,
    My heart no longer burns;
My sight to common shops and streets
    With clearer optics turns.

But still I sing through Ludgate Hill,
    Beat on, old heart, for ever,

And send thy life through all the streets
　　That border on the river—

That hang upon old Thames's tide,
　　And line his banks afar,
With all the leagues that run to east
　　And west of Temple Bar—

Send thy best blood through them, stout heart,
　　Beat 'neath a million suns,
And write for cities yet unborn
　　The valiant tale that runs

Through every vein of thy rich life,
　　And flushes all thy story—
The grand old tale how, Duty led
　　Our English sons to glory.

Ring out from thy fair steeple still,
　　The sweet old bells of Bow,
And with their chimes made sweeter yet,
　　May their old legend grow!

So when thy thousands meet to shout
　　Around each new Lord Mayor,
Our children's children's eyes may still
　　See Whittington sit there.

Send still thy roaring ocean down
　　The tide of Charing Cross,
And let its currents, surging round
　　The Abbey lintels, toss,

While cannon's roar, and belfry's rock,
    And kerchiefs' foam on high,
And waving hats, and loud huzzas
    Proclaim the Queen is nigh.

O wondrous city !—wondrous land !
    To which we owe our birth ;
None ever rose so queenlike on
    The old Homeric earth.

Old Greece's purple skies ne'er shone
    Upon a clime like ours ;
Hymettus stored not herbs so sweet
    As are our English flowers.

The Grecian valleys feed not sheep
    With wool so closely curled ;
The Grecian steeds were not like ours,
    The racers of the world.

Bright Athens once unrivalled wore
    Her boasted violet crown ;
As village unto city is,
    So was she to our town.

Vienna, Paris, Berlin, Rome,
    Each city merits praise ;
Give London seven wondering years,
    Give them their fair nine days.

I vow that such allotment meets
    Each city's merits duly ;

But should you plead for more, then take
  Nine days in June or July.

Thus rhyming in my study close,
  I strung the careless lines together,
The while beyond my window rose
  The sob and sough of winter weather;
The while from storms that swept each street
  (Like birds blown inwards to their cage)
My fancies flying homewards fleet,
  Sought refuge from the winter's rage
With fire stirred bright, and lighted gas,
  I by the contrast bade defiance
To all the night could bring to pass,
  With storm, and rain, in joint alliance;
And as I snugly glanced about,
  And drew me nearer to the fender,
The blaze from fire and gas streamed out,
  And lent my little room a splendour.
Shone ancient lustre of the oak,
  Fell crimson curtains fold on fold,
Bright vistas down the mirrors broke,
  And fires burnt bright within the gold,
And from the floor to ceiling rose,
  In stately piling, shelf on shelf,
Behind the glass, in long-drawn rows,
  The books that are my second self.

THE "STORY WITHOUT AN END."

Far adown the vista leading
  To the dim and distant years,
I can see a child still reading,
  In earshot of comrades' cheers.
They are 'neath the window playing,
  He is hid 'neath curtain's shade;
With a mystic comrade straying
  Through the darkling woodland glade.
Brothers, sisters, earnest seeking,
  Loudly call, "What, are you lost?"
He replies not to their speaking,
  He is deaf as any post.
He is deaf to all their pleading,
  And will sit till shadows blending;
Take him to the lamplight reading
  Still that—Story without Ending

Of the child with his dark blue eyes,
  Bluer from the violet's gaze;
Deeper from the message sent them,
  On the starlight's slender rays.
Full of love and secrets told him,
  By the purple dragonfly;
In the hour when caves enfold him,
  And the busy spiders ply
All their skill in curtain-weaving,
  Drawing close a friendly shade

Round the little wanderer leaving
  Sudden darkness of the glade,

Where his eager footsteps led him
  From his little hut astray;
Learning all the mysteries taught him
  By the water on his way.
Till from every corner fading,
  Swift and swifter went the light;
And the wind with its upbraiding,
  Rose upon the lonely night.

Then we two sought shelter gladly,
  In the cavern's safe recess;
For to us all sounded sadly,
  In the wooded wilderness.
And the fireflies trooping round us,
  Light with tapers all the cave;
And the harebells blithely sound us,
  Sending forth their sweetest stave.

Thus by night in caverns resting,
  And by day in gardens roving,
Shared I ever in his questing,
  Loved the insects of his loving.
And my childhood crowned with roses,
  And the myrtle's fragrant blending,
Seems to glow a bright oasis,
  That, alas! has had an ending.

And, indeed, I hear wise voices,
    Utter sage their prophecy
O'er the childhood that rejoices
    In such stories' mystery.
" Nay, we grudge you not your myrtle,
    Very soon you found the real ;
Bitter blast and thunder's hurtle,
    Swept the lines of your ideal
World of wandering and adventure,
    With the child beneath the night,
And your after peradventure
    Paid the price of its delight."
Was it so, indeed?   I think not,
    For my life has happy been,
Sipping pleasures none said, "drink not,"
    And delight has been its queen.
Still that happy past has faded,
    And my childhood's world o'erthrown ;
I can sit no longer shaded
    By the curtain's fold alone.
And though brilliant years I reckon,
    Marked by many a gay success,
And I still see Fortune beckon
    Me along to happiness,
I would still give without measure,
    Pleasures past and onwards tending,
To take back my childhood's pleasure,
    In that Story without Ending.

O tales that keep close in your pages,
　The better half of all my days;
O tales that are my friends and sages,
　Dear tales I scarce may dare to praise.
For words that I can coin must be
　Such tame and feeble words to tell
What dear and loving friends to me,
　Your legends loved so long and well.

THE TALES OF THE EAST.

When a child I was a traveller
　Into many distant lands,
Went I wending with the pilgrims
　O'er the desert's dreary sands;
Saw the domes of Eastern cities
　'Mid the stately palm-trees rise,
Saw the myriad mosques of Bagdad
　Cut against the purple skies;
Yet my England, mother England, still I dwelt upon
　thy shore,
Patient student 'neath the lamplight of the bright
　Arabian lore.
　　Tales of wonder, tales of beauty,
　　　How my child heart's eager burning,
　　Kept me captive to your pages,
　　　To the loss of deeper learning!

In the winter 'neath the lamplight,
    In the summer on the sward,
Kept me morn, and noon, and even,
    From all childhood's sport debarred.
How could I who went with princes, where the
    wondrous genii were,
Wake to join in meaner pastime such as other children
    share ?
    Cease, my brothers, cease your calling,
        I am at the mystic cave
    With the wretch who hath forgotten
        The one word his life can save.
    Faint, my sisters, come your voices,
        As I tread the marble floors
    Of that palace by the lake's side,
        With its twice three hundred doors.
Hark, now, the earth is shaking, and the thunder peals
    around,
As I sink with young Aladdin through the yawning of
    the ground.
    There I see the jewels glistening,
        Like rich fruits on every tree ;
    I am in the magic garden,
        All your voices lost on me.
    Topaz, diamond, sapphire, gleaming,
        With the ruby's red starlight,
    Shed their radiance through the alleys
        Of that garden of delight.

I would dream away existence, on its banks and 'neath
    its trees,
But Aladdin waves me onward, where the magic lamp
    he sees.

    See the palace swiftly rises,
        On the magic of its basements ;
    See the sunlight answered duly
        From its four-and-twenty casements.
    See the garden's joyous treasures,
        Borne by slaves in swift succession ;
    See the streets of Canton filling
        With the pomp of his procession.
    See the bride is borne in triumph
        To the palace of her lover,
    Hark ! the Afrite with his new lamps,
        Seeks the old lamp to discover.

So in fancy went I travelling, out of call of comrades
    playing,
Willing loser of their pastime, with the young Aladdin
    straying.

    Or on Autumn noontides lying,
        With my book upon the sands,
    I dreamed the sea was murmuring
        On the beach of other lands.
    Saw the rich Balsoran merchants
        Bring their bales to wait the breeze ;
    Saw the sloop of Sindbad sailing,
        In the smile of sunlit seas.

Saw the treacherous island floating like a meadow on
    the deep;
Saw the grooms of King Mihrage, near the mare their
    vigils keep.
      Then I started fresh with Sindbad,
        From the rivers of Bagdad;
      Never merchant on his voyage,
        More compliant partner had.
      With him I lingered sleeping,
        'Neath the noontide shade of trees;
      With him I woke deserted
        By the ship gone with the breeze.
      With him I climbed the palm-tree,
        And gazing far around
    Saw the roc's egg rising whitely,
        Like a hillock from the ground.
Saw the swoop of snowy pinions, as they circled clear
    and clearer;
Saw the wondrous roc come sailing, sailing nearer still
    and nearer.
      Oh! the night that I went roaming
        With Khosrouschah, the Sultan;
      When the fallen night had shut well
        Each house with bar and bolt in.
      How we spied the lamplight gleaming
        Through a crevice in the door,
    And by words we caught made curious.
      Listening, lingering to catch more.

How we laughed at those three sisters choosing
    husbands in their sport,
One the butcher, one the baker, one the Lord of
    Persia's court!
      See the doe is fleeting swiftly,
        Through the woodland's dim recesses:
      See the monarch madly spurring
        On her track still eager presses.
      Now the night has darkened round him,
        And the doe is far in flight,
      When the magic palace blazes,
        And the thickets gleam with light.
Enters he 'mid perfumed odours, and the blaze of gold
    brocade ;
There, 'mid sixty beauteous damsels, sits the bright
    enchanted maid.
      Through the night in dreams returning,
        Came these wonders ever blending ;
      Lamps 'neath stately domes were burning,
        Smoke in monstrous shapes ascending.
      Curtains waving back would show me
        Some bright vision at the casement ;
      Or the dark of woods bestow me
        Mansions lit from roof to basement.
Caliphs, genii, and ghouls, viziers, slaves. and
    Barmecide,
Satisfied my sleep with visions, till I woke again to
    read.

Close the bright Arabian volumes,
  Turn to boyhood's dearer page;
To the young romantic heroes,
  Of that young romantic age.

THE WAVERLEY NOVELS.

Ah! but turning now to gaze me
  Where some forty volumes lie,
Some swift memory seems to place me
  Where all changes suddenly;
Sweet my mother's voice sounds reading,
  While a child leans on her knee,
At each pause attempted pleading,
  " More of that tale's mystery."

'Tis of Halbert she is reading,
  And fair Mary Avenel,
And the ghostly white receding
  Of the Ladye at the well.
Oh! dear mother, years have vanished
  Since you read that tale to me;
But from memory never banished,
  Still returns its mystery.

Dearest mother, all my boyhood
  Owed of tender love to thee,
From the kiss pressed on the forehead,
  Of my helpless infancy,

To the lesson subtly chosen,
  Less a task than a delight;
When the winter even closing,
  Brought the pleasant winter night.

Then, by lamp and candle lighted,
  Sat we with the book before us,
Had we seen, then, second-sighted,
  All the years that would pass o'er us?
Thou wert then a girl light-hearted,
  Younger then than I am now,
Six-and-twenty years have parted
  Us from youth, and with their snow

Have drifted swiftly o'er our journey,
  Changing youth, and face, and heart;
Neither now in life's gay tourney
  Could as then take jocund part;
And the volumes lie unaltered,
  But were we to read again,
Could we bear the voice that faltered
  O'er the old familiar strain?

Dear ones loved since then are sleeping
  Their last sleep beneath the mould;
Year by year the years are sweeping
  Us the nearer to their fold;
Yet all rises clear before me,
  Room, and book, and candlelight,
And your loving face bends o'er me
  As it were but yesternight.

Six-and-twenty years have changed us,
  As they change all earthly things,
Yet not once have they estranged us,
  Each to each as fondly clings
As when both felt all the gladness
  That the May of lifetime brings
To the heart, ere time and sadness
  Break the once elastic springs.

Madre Mia, years in passing
  Throw their care and throw their shade,
And the present's mirror glassing,
  Shows the havoc they have made;
Yet, indeed, to me in seeming
  You are scarcely older now
Than when from my childhood's dreaming,
  I looked on your girlish brow.

Youth has lingered so to gift thee
  With its beauty and its laughter,
While my years have travelled swiftly,
  Catching thine that they ran after,
Till it seems to-day has brought us,
  Matched in equal age and heart,
And whatever Time has wrought us,
  I have had the double part.

Could I look on those romances,
  Read in boyhood's merry time,
And not cast these backward glances,
  And not seek to fix in rhyme

Some faint record, some poor measure,
    Some fond image of the past,
That when I am dead may treasure
    Thy dear memory in it glassed?

But I pause on looking round me
    At the shelves book-laden rising,
At the volumes that have bound me
    With their legends fond enticing,
Lest I add one to their number,
    While my heart its favourites sums;
For as memory wakes from slumber,
    Volume following volume comes;
All that childhood loves to live in,
    World of fairy tales enchanting,
Legends of the Champions Seven,
    And the famous Bean-stalk's planting;
Novel after novel linking
    Time's long past unto the present,
Mistress Aphra Behn's strong drinking
    To the modern taste unpleasant;
Edgeworth's safe tea-table flavour—
    Tea that's strong and wholesome too;
Fielding with his racy savour
    Of the naughty things men do;
Richardson's immortal writings,
    They, at least, can never hurt you,
Since they all are but incitings
    To the practice of pure virtue;

Yet the other day perusing
    Pamela's instructive letters,
She seemed really introducing
    Certain somewhat ticklish matters;
But let who will gibing, jesting,
    Snatch from Pamela her bays,
Matchless beyond all contesting
    Is divine Clarissa's praise,
Finest type romance has given
    Of a fair and gracious woman,
Till through suffering raised to heaven—
    Till by wrong made more than human;
There is Smollett's Humphrey Clinker—
    There is Burney's Evelina—
There, though writ by a wise thinker,
    Is a volume I would screen a
Little in the corner, lurking
    Out of ken of eyes suspicious,
Lest it tempt the evil smirking
    Of some saintly mouth malicious;
There the modern novels greet me,
    Of all shape, and form, and fashion,
Ever puzzling as they meet me,
    Bought at random how to match in,—
Not like the old novels ranging
    In trim line a hundred strong,
A firm phalanx and unchanging,
    Set in brotherhood along;—

There are Lytton's lordly volumes,
   Bathed in purple of his dreaming,
E'en in glancing down their columns,
   Seem rich rubies redly gleaming,
And the rubies and the jewels,
   And the crimson of his diction,
Garb in pomp like bright Ithuriels,
   The young heroes of his fiction—
Garb in pomp the scholar's wooing
   Of majestic Madeline ;
And Maltravers' wild pursuing
   Of one vision through all scene,
Till at last, when day is setting—
   Summer's day, and day of life—
He meets, claims the unforgetting,
   Long-lost Alice for his wife ;
While his women, who can match you,
   Lytton's pure and calm ideal ?
Like the snow-white classic statue,
   Flushing, warming to the real,
Ranging 'gainst the crimson colour
   Of his warm, impassioned prose,
Breathed upon by Venus' scholar,
   Each fair form to woman glows.
There the poets with their chimings
   Or of golden Greece or Rome,
Or the sweet, familiar rhymings
   Of the English hearth and home,

Range from Æschylus and Homer—
 Range from ten times dearer Virgil,
To young Swinburne, sweetest comer,
 In whose ears the murmurs surge still
Of the foam round Ocean's daughters,
 Who young Hylas safely keep,
Of the lap of Lesbian waters,
 Drifting dark o'er Sappho's sleep;
Him whom Juno must have cradled,
 Or fair Venus on Mount Ida,
Scarce by Christians was he swaddled
 Ere the old gods swept aside a
Corner of the curtains, hanging
 O'er the Pagan child's repose,
And to Bacchante cymbals clanging,
 He to great Olympus rose;
Where but on Jove's mount, and with him,
 Learnt he those sonorous songs,
Or where caught that classic rhythm,
 That to Greece by right belongs?
There are Taylor, Bailey, Browning,
 There, too, Browning's noble wife,
All her Florence laurels crowning,
 Less than England's love her life—
There is lone, love-laden Landon
 Singing sweet her Sapphic strains,
While the waves the solemn sand on
 Breaking, far on Afric's plains

See the grave where she is sleeping,
　Far from all beloved ones lying—
She who through her latest weeping,
　Listened still for their replying—
There Keats, oh! perfumes how divine,
　Of lilies and of heliotropes,
And fragrant bowl of spicèd wine,
　And saffron meads on sunny slopes,
And glimpse of maids on winter eve,
　Dim haloed in the moon's cold light,
Listing to strains that lovers leave,
　Still stealing round the frost-bound night :
And Tennyson with setting suns,
　That sink with lurid light o'er plains
Of level Lincoln, while there runs
　A sough of sorrow through the strains,
Like the low wind, that rising, sighs
　All night along those marshy miles,
Till, with a clang, his music flies
　To lovers' laughs and ladies' smiles ;
Ah! thus still ye lure me onward,
　Volume after volume claiming,
As my gaze runs upward, downward,
　I can scarcely cease from naming
Dear companions of my childhood,
　Dearer friends of later years,
Calmers of my stern or wild mood,
　Soothers of my saddest tears ;

But as one who through a garden
  Walketh, singing ever gay,
Sudden pauses where the margin
  Shows a precipice that way,
So to me the margin sloping
  From the present's happy scene,
Scarce can yield me longer hoping
  Of repeating what has been ;
Who knows what the future brings me,
  Change of time, and change of weather,
When the hearts, now linking with me,
  Shall have ceased to chime together—
When the volumes that now bind me
  Can be hardly gazed upon,
As the bitter tears will blind me,
  Thinking of the loved ones gone ;
But if God shall will it e'en so,
  That such sorrow must be given,
And His will should be to wean so
  All my thoughts from earth to heaven,
Still, oh Father, through all sorrow,
  May I think of what has been,
Through the dark of that to-morrow,
  Keeping still "my memory green."

THE OLDEN DAYS.

" The spacious times of great Elizabeth."
TENNYSON.

'Tis by the present's purple light
    We read all ancient story ;
'Tis from that light the olden days
    Take more than half their glory.

'Tis our romance which lights the torch,
    Whose blaze falls brightest there ;
'Tis we who blow the silver trump
    That echoes through that air.

The men who lived within that past,
    Transfigured to our eyes,
Could we show them our fancy's sketch,
    Would fail to recognise

Our brilliant picture as the cold
    And barren life they led ;
And they would point us backward still,
    And calling on the dead,

Would say, "Behold the golden age,
    Shines far behind us there ;
There are the horns of fairy land,
    And there the haunted air !

" There are the heroes that you sing,
    The women that you praise ;
That is the land of old renown,
    And those the famous days."

So future ages, looking back
  Upon this age of ours,
Will hear heroic trumpets blow,
  And see Arcadian bowers—

Will speak of us as great and good,
  Men of an ampler time,
Whose names shall pass from age to age,
  Rolled on the poet's rhyme.

LAYS OF THE HOME AFFECTIONS.

TO MRS. FLETCHER, OF KILLOUGHTER.

THE ceaseless sound of London life
  Pours in upon my ear;
And yet 'tis not its revelry
  My spirit seems to hear.

No—other memories stir within
  The heart's remotest cell;
The bell that rings from yon old church,
  Seems now no common bell.*

Sweet snatches of old music come
  Upon each scattered chime,
That tune themselves to hope and prayer,
  Meet music for the rhyme,

* St. James's. Piccadilly.

Whose words are now too sudden snatched,
　For polish or for wit;
Those hurried prayers affection breathes,
　Fast coined and faster writ.

But you will take with ample grace,
　The tribute of my verse;
And say, as once you sweetly said,
　" For better or for worse."

It matters not that here a line
　Or syllable may jar;
The value lies not in the words,
　But where the feelings are.

And now o'er thee the new year bends,
　With soft and smiling skies,
And storms that sweep aside from arms
　Where gently cradled lies

That nursling of a few short weeks,
　That claims so large a part—
No less division than a third
　Share in a mother's heart.

So happy are you smiling o'er
　The babe you closely press;
You think it matters little now,
　A good wish more or less.

And yet good wishes ever wait
　Upon the opening year;

And so I venture timidly
　To breathe one in your ear.

May never Graces famed of old,
　Be fairer than this child ;
Nor sweeter face than hers have e'er
　From Reynolds' canvas smiled.

Nor e'en those sisters* whom I praised
　As passing all of grace ;
That e'er before or since has charmed
　In English maiden's face,

Glow from Sir Joshua's cunning hand
　More brightly than we'll see,
In years to come, thou little one,
　Thy mother's face in thee,

Who to the present age repeats
　The charms that painted well,
The ivory we have treasured shows,
　Used in her mother dwell.

And be thou yet another link
　In that transmitted line
Of loveliness, that still through all
　Thy mother's race shall shine.

I would say more, but moments fly,
　And I would fain my lay

---

* " The Waldegrave Nieces," in the Strawberry Hill Collection.

Should greet thy mother as she wakes
    Upon her natal day.

Then go, my verse, though faulty all,
    Though jangled out of tune ;
Yet greet her kindly, and say soft,
    " He hopes an answer soon."

MARY'S TURKEY.

" Michael's turkey—Michael's turkey."

LAST night we feasted well, I ween,
    The board was nobly spread,
We brought good tempers free from spleen.
    And grace was duly said ;
But soup and fish just tasted went
    (Our thoughts had gone before),
When, lo! we caught a savoury scent
    En arant through the door ;
Then covers raised, the fumes began
    In odorous wreaths to spread,
As ham of York at foot was seen,
    And turkey at the head ;
The *entrées* handed round in vain,
    We let them swiftly go,
'Twas very plain each other dish
    Was but sent up for show ;

We viewed them with the same disdain
    We might have viewed beef *charqui,*
And with united onslaught rushed
    To feast on Mary's turkey.

How plump it looked, the cover raised,
    How tempting, rich, and brown!
Now knife and fork in air are poised,
    And now fall swiftly down,
A slice clean taken off the breast,
    Another and another,
With savoury sausage by their side,
    And savoury sauce to smother;
What matter that the winds blow loud,
    The outside weather murky,
While we sit at the lighted board,
    And feast on Mary's turkey?

Soup *à la reine* I envy not,
    Nor *Creey,* nor *bonne femme,*
While on my plate I lay a slice
    Of that crisp Yorkshire ham;
Let seasons change, and fashions too,
    But 'midst all change of weather,
Let ham and turkey undivorced
    Be sausage-chained together.
Another help I vow I'll have,
    Digestive organs work ye,
O help me now in feeding thus
    On Mary's farm-yard turkey!

Let Frenchmen praise their *sole Normande*,
  And English haunch of venison,
On neither dainty dish to-day
  Do I bestow a benison ;
Nor *sauce tomate*, nor *sauce Soubise*,
  Where unsuspected lurk ye,
Dear onion atoms can seduce
  My taste from Mary's turkey.

O *riz de veau* to pot may go,
  And eke *petits croustades*,
And *mayonnaise* and *vol au vent*,
  Suprême and *marinade ;*
E'en native joints of noblest fame—
  Ay, e'en the great sirloin
Wage battle with unequal force
  When ham and turkey join ;
All honour to thy native farm,
  And younger brethren stalk ye,
Till each full crop in size may cope
  With crop of this roast turkey !

E'en Chateaubriand's famous *filet*,
  Though served by Dudley's *chef*,
Would not find us its victims silly,
  Would from our forks be safe ;
For we who sneered at Jeames's offer
  Of *potage reine* and *bisque*,
To us Chevet, l'otel might proffer
  Tout ce, qu'il y a, sans risque,

Of *comestibles* as a gift,
　　Nor tempt us feasted sinners,
Full-blown and reckless of the fate
　　Of any future dinners.

An Irish farm-yard fed this bird,
　　Who, saved from feeding Fenians,
In dear old London is served up,
　　And robbed of breast and pinions.
Take, take his honoured bones away,
　　But not to tomb or urn,
For two good legs like his, I swear,
　　Shall serve another turn.
O, generous bird! right nobly thou
　　Hast feasted me to-day,
And such good service I but ill
　　With meagre verse repay.
No niggard thou, who dare say nay,
　　May "wicked Fenians" dirk ye,
A nobler bird was never stuffed
　　Than Mary's farm-yard turkey.

And to the liberal hand that sent,
　　What thanks can I send back?
O, may her farm-yard flourish still,
　　And never turkeys lack—
And may they strut and gobble still
　　Through many a coming year,
And every now and then may one
　　Display his plumage here!

May peace and plenty round her reign,
  Nor Fenians dare to lurk ye
Within a hundred leagues of where
  Struts Mary's farm-yard turkey.

BIRTHDAY STANZAS.

TO T. C. M.

November 4th, 1867.

Now glancing at the *Times*, set forth
  Upon my breakfast-table,
I start to see November four
  Beyond the reach of fable.

November four again, then let
  Again the song be sung ;
Let household bells, and household glees,
  To welcome it give tongue.

Since last I wrote, some bloom has left
  Alike the heart and cheek ;
Perchance we now less gleeful feel,
  Perchance less gleeful speak.

But yet this change, if change there be,
  Has scarcely come too soon ;
For then it was Life's April-time,
  And now it is Life's June.

But all Spring's sunshine, all her tears,
    I never could compare
To that repose of summer calm,
    Which golden June-tides wear.

The crown serene of womanhood,
    And manhood's summer prime,
Seem risen to a loftier height,
    And need a nobler rhyme

Than any strain boy-rhymers send,
    Or verses maidens bring,
To deck with lays as light as it,
    The light capricious spring.

And would that I might sing to-day,
    Some full and ample strain;
Some swelling stanza that should ring
    In echoes o'er again,

To tell the high romantic tale,
    The years may well demand,
Of wanderings far through many a scene
    Of many a foreign land.

Since last I sang, the Elbe has met
    Our gaze of glad surprise;
And Dresden's galleries have unrolled
    Their treasures to our eyes.

A country home I seem to see,
    'Mid German pastures stand,

Around Bohemia's hills look on
The Kaiser's Vaterland.

There gracious Herr, and gracious Frau,
For us spread plenteous cheer;
There flowed the famous Rhenish wine,
And there the Bairisch beer.

We've seen the midnight stars come out,
O'er Berlin's level plain;
And greeted the glad harvest moon,
At Frankfort-on-the-Maine—

Have seen the sunset fade at eve
Along the Leman lake;
And watched the conclaved Alps group round,
Stern mourners at his wake,

At Florence stood by Arno's side,
And marked the golden quiver
Her thousand lamps sent down at night
To light her radiant river,

While Florence skies were powdered o'er
With stars of that rich night,
That clustered round the Apennines,
And bathed each purple height

Of that fair city, Beauty's queen,
Queen-rose of all the earth;
Though London be supreme o'er all,
In majesty and worth.

At Rome, have wandered dismal through
   Her charnel-haunts of death,
With listless step and sinking heart,
   Drank in her tainted breath;

Then gladly saw 'neath moonlight rise
   Fair Milan's glorious shrine;
That wondrous dream of architect,
   Wrought into form divine.

Then silently by night we stole,
   Upon a watery waste;
A dark strange figure at the stern,
   Drove on our barge in haste.

We drifted on through some strange dream,
   Of cities of the dead;
Beneath us coiled the channels dark,
   Dark was the sky o'erhead.

Dim funeral lights shone few and far,
   And from the water grew
Dark labyrinths of streets, and lines
   Of houses stole to view.

Such—as we stand, and backward gaze,
   Are scenes that thickly rise;
Bright as the colours of romance,
   And pleasant in our eyes.

And proud Vienna's ancient walls,
   And Munich's stately street;

And Stoltzenfels and Eberstein,
    Again our vision meet.

Then nearer still our backward gaze
    Falls on familiar ways ;
The pleasant summer paths where still,
    The English dweller strays.

On Dover, Hastings, Devon's shores,
    On many a cliff and haven ;
And where through Warwick's fertile woods,
    Winds on our Shakespeare's Avon.

Until we reach our London home,
    Where calmly now I sing;
Trusting such memories still for us
    The coming years may bring.

But see, as still I wistful look,
    The evening shades fall round ;
November's surly eve comes forth,
    And shrouds the dimming ground.

Then let us rise, our survey o'er,
    And face the future time,
Whose prophecy points still for us,
    To many a pleasant clime.

Let us rejoice, as is most right,
    In days of summer prime ;
Its own peculiar beauty still,
    God gives to every time.

Then let us rise, and onward go,
  With hearts of bravest trust;
No standing still—when Time speeds on,
  Willing or not, we must.

MEMORIES OF CHILDHOOD.

TO T. C. M.

What shall I sing to thee, my sister dear,
  In that slow measure that thou lovest best?
Shall I go back, retracing year by year,
  And, pilgrim-like, at all old shrines take rest?
Methinks that journey were too slow and long,
  Even to suit a measure such as this;
But come with me, and we will walk, in song,
  Through scattered scenes of well-remembered bliss.

The misty steam is mantling over all
  The dark green hedges with a vaporous breath,
And the wild woodbines' yellow trumpets fall,
  Heavy with dew, upon the grass beneath;
The fair field flowers swift are closing every eye,
  That starlike shone one little hour ago;
The stars themselves are weaving soft and sly
  Their golden fringe on evening's furbelow;

With drooping necks and meek reclining heads,
  On dewy meads the wearied kine find rest,

While through the darkling mist that evening sheds,
  The corn-crake crieth from her distant nest ;
The latest cart-load staggers from the field,
  Fragrant with heap of freshly-tedded hay,
Mingling with odours bean and clover yield,
  The parting incense of a summer day.

Again an eve of still and soft repose,
  Where twilight broodeth o'er our childhood's world,
The amber sunset in the heaven glows,
  Her crimson banners has the west unfurled :
The water-hen skims swiftly o'er the pond,
  Whose sedgy banks are lined by water-flags,
And stealing through the hush that reigns beyond,
  The river ripples over mimic crags.

How dear to us were then the stream and bird !
  How many an eve we lingered on that ground,
The running water through the silence heard,
  The sole sweet talker in the calm around ;
Sometimes we sought, with venturous feet, to go
  O'er stepping-stones that bridged the deepening
    stream ;
Ah ! time since then, swift as its waters flow,
  Has drifted by us, making all a dream.

The dear old garden round our country home,
  The fields and paddocks spreading far around
The wood's recesses, where we used to roam,
  And dream ourselves on some enchanter's ground—

All—all rise clearly on my memory now,
    And with them, through quick tears there rises too
The vision of our sister's sunny brow,
    Her bounding steps, and glancing eyes' bright blue—

Her golden hair, now sullied in the grave—
    Her glad, fresh laughter that will ring no more—
Her mirth, that to our sports new relish gave;
    'Tis hard to think all these for ever o'er—
'Tis hard to think that she so loved is gone—
    That she so young is sleeping in the dust—
That we are now upon the earth so lone,
    So few to love us, few to love or trust.

IN MEMORY OF M. S. F.

*Died Christmas Day, 1867. Written January 4th, 1868, her
Birthday.*

No more to thee the birthday lay—
    No more the words of praise ;
O Death, we feel thy victory
    O'er all our household ways.

Fled is thy sting, indeed, for her,
    But oh, to us most keen,
As we recall the happy past,
    And think what might have been.

My own bright sister! how my heart
  Sinks low, and dull, and drear;
How more than twenty years of life
  Have died with the dead year.

The jest, the mirth, that made me still
  A boy, in heart, at least,
Struck dead for ever as they rose
  To greet the Christmas feast.

I ne'er again shall speak the words
  I often spoke in glee;
All old familiar jests are lost
  In bitter thoughts of thee.

Our little band is broken now,
  And by the gap we stand,
And miss the dear familiar touch
  Of one dear sister's hand.

I never thought that sorrow could
  O'ertake us in this guise,
That thou wouldst be the first to pass
  For ever from our eyes.

I never thought of death and thee—
  Thou hadst no part in death;
So happy went thy eager heart.
  So full of life thy breath.

I fed the coming year with dreams—
  The light dreams of a boy,

Of happy meetings in thy home,
    And with a secret joy

I thought how I would bring my verse,
    My task of the gone year,
And read to thee my favourite lines—
    Lines thou wilt never hear.

And not a line I wrote but still
    Thy smile shone bright along;
I heard thee read, in fancy, words
    Turned by thy voice to song.

For many a month my heart was fed
    With thoughts of glad surprise,
When sent a gift of coming spring
    My book should greet thine eyes,

Where meanings should be clear to thee,
    By others only guessed,
As here and there the verses glanced
    At some familiar jest.

We had so many dear, our hearts
    Had twined for years together;
Alas! for life's bright vanished days
    And for its April weather.

We shared them both, we hardly knew
    A serious grief or care;
How many a ghost of pleasures rise,
    In which we both had share!

Now I have kissed thy lips in death,
  Beside thy grave have knelt;
O, can I e'er dream as I dreamt,
  Or feel as I have felt?

No ; dead with thee the eager scheme,
  The future's ardent plan ;
Last year beheld a boy in heart,
  This sees a saddened man.

And now my task has lost its charm,
  But since 'tis finished, take,
Dear sister, to thy memory all
  I once wrote for thy sake.

Upon thy tomb I lay the gift
  I meant to please thee living ;
But oh how changed is the bright dream
  Once cherished of the giving!

RANKEN AND CO., PRINTERS, DRURY HOUSE, ST. MARY-LE-STRAND, LONDON.

CAROLS OF COCKAYNE.

BY HENRY S. LEIGH.

(*Vers de Société, and charming Verses descriptive of London life.*)

With numerous exquisite little designs by ALFRED CONCANNEN.

In preparation, small 4to. elegant.

Now ready, Price 3s. 6d.

THE PROMETHEUS BOUND OF ÆSCHYLUS.

Translated in the Original Metres by C. B. CAYLEY, B.A.

" This new translation will, we doubt not, be warmly welcomed as ably carrying out the object which the writer seeks to achieve—that of familiarising English readers, through the medium of their own language, with the stately forms and the scientific principles of the Greek versification. In this, as well as in preserving the spirit of the original, the writer has eminently succeeded."—OBSERVER.

Now ready, 4to, 10s. 6d., on toned paper, very elegant.

BIANCA: POEMS AND BALLADS.

BY EDWARD BRENNAN.

MR. EDMUND OLLIER'S POEMS,

This day, cloth neat, 5s.

POEMS FROM THE GREEK MYTHOLOGY,

AND MISCELLANEOUS POEMS.

BY EDMUND OLLIER.

" What he has written is enough, and more than enough, to give him a high rank amongst the most successful cultivators of the English Muse."—GLOBE.

This day, crown 8vo., Price 7s. 6d. ; by post, 8s.

POEMS:

CHARACTERISTIC, ITINERARY, AND MISCELLANEOUS.

BY P. F. ROE.

Part I.—Rythmical Etchings of Character. II.—Tracings of Travel. III.—Minor Poems. IV.—Translations.

London : JOHN CAMDEN HOTTEN, 74 & 75, Piccadilly.

THE NEW POETICAL SATIRE.

HORSE & FOOT; OR, PILGRIMS TO PARNASSUS.

"I'll not march through Coventry with them that's flat."

Crown 8vo. Price 3s. 6d.

"It is understood in literary circles that a new poem of very considerable power, sharply criticising the peculiarities of modern verse, is about to be published. The author is spoken of as an Oxford graduate, and a man of mark amongst members of the University, who look forward to his book making some sensation in the reading world."—STANDARD.

"Whatever may be thought of this spirited satire of 841 lines, no one will accuse its writer of personality; and however hard he may hit some of the literati of the day, he appears to write in perfect good faith, and, in thus frankly avowing his own critical convictions, to be influenced but by one thought—the healthy interests of English literature. Without acquaintance with those mentioned in his pages, 'or indeed with any one in the literary world,' Mr. Crawley writes 'independently,' and for this moral courage we thank him."

In 4to., exquisitely printed on ivory paper, elegant binding, Price 10s. 6d.

PUCK ON PEGASUS.

A New Edition, twice the size of the old one, with many New Poems, and Additional Illustrations by Sir Noel Paton, Millais, John Tenniel, Richard Doyle, M. Ellen Edwards, and other distinguished Artists.

This day, in crown 8vo., toned paper, elegant, Price 3s. 6d.

WIT & HUMOUR.

By the "Autocrat of the Breakfast Table."

A volume of delightfully humorous Poems, very similar to the mirthful verses of Tom Hood. Readers will not be disappointed with this work.

OLD ENGLISH RELIGIOUS BALLADS AND CAROLS.

This day, in small 4to., with very beautiful floriated borders, in the Renaissance style.

SONGS OF THE NATIVITY.

An entirely new collection of Old Carols, including some never before given in any collection. With Music to the more popular. Edited by W. H. HUSK, Librarian to the Sacred Harmonic Society. In charmingly appropriate cloth, gilt, and admirably adapted for binding in antique calf, or morocco, 12s. 6d.

"A volume which will not be without peculiar interest to lovers of ancient English poetry, and to admirers of our National Sacred Music. The work forms a handsome square 8vo., and has been printed with beautiful floriated borders by Whittingham and Wilkins. The Carols embrace the joyous and festive songs of the olden time, as well as those sacred melodies which have maintained their popularity from a period long before the Reformation."

This day, fcap. 8vo., 7s. 6d.

STRAWBERRY HILL; AND OTHER POEMS.

By COLBURN MAYNE, Esq.

Shortly, elegantly printed.

THE VILLAGE ON THE FORTH; AND OTHER POEMS.

By PHILIP LATIMER.

London: JOHN CAMDEN HOTTEN, 74 & 75, Piccadilly.

www.ingramcontent.com/pod-product-compliance
Lightning Source LLC
Chambersburg PA
CBHW060610030726
47498CB00005B/1620